SHOOTOUT!

The counterfeiters broke out of hiding abruptly, going all directions at once. Longarm spotted a couple of them coming toward him, guns in their hands.

"Throw down those pistols!" Longarm bellowed. "This is the law!"

The counterfeiters ignored the order and jerked their guns upward.

That was exactly the reaction Longarm had expected. His .44 was already leveled, and he fired twice before either of the men could get off a shot. The slugs bored into their chests, throwing them back so they disappeared into the clouds of dust again.

The next man came shooting . . .

D1516171

DON'T MISS THESE
ALL-ACTION WESTERN SERIES
FROM THE BERKLEY PUBLISHING GROUP

◄► TABOR EVANS ◄►

LONGARM

AND THE
RACY LADIES

J

JOVE BOOKS, NEW YORK

LONGARM AND THE RACY LADIES

A Jove Book / published by arrangement with
the author

PRINTING HISTORY
Jove edition / October 1996

The Putnam Berkley World Wide Web site address is
http://www.berkley.com/berkley

ISBN: 0-515-11956-3

A JOVE BOOK®
Jove Books are published by The Berkley Publishing Group,
200 Madison Avenue, New York, New York 10016.
JOVE and the "J" design are trademarks
belonging to Jove Publications, Inc.

PRINTED IN THE UNITED STATES OF AMERICA

10 9 8 7 6 5 4 3 2 1

Chapter 1

Longarm lowered the newspaper to his lap and used the left sleeve of his brown tweed coat to wipe away the fine beads of sweat that had popped out on his forehead. He told himself he was sweating because the lobby of the hotel was hot tonight. It wasn't quite ten o'clock, and the heat from a summer afternoon in New Mexico wouldn't completely fade away until after midnight. So it couldn't be a case of nerves making him sweat.

Surely not.

The big federal lawman was sitting in the lobby of one of the best hotels in Albuquerque. He had ridden down on the train from Denver earlier in the day and met the man he was supposed to contact this evening. Jim Harrelson was a United States deputy marshal, too. At the moment, Harrelson was sitting on the other side of the lobby, wearing a derby hat and a suit with a loud, garish check. He looked like the whiskey drummer he was pretending to be, right down to the reddish nose of a man who too often sampled the wares he was supposed to be selling. That wasn't a clever bit of camouflage, Longarm knew; Harrelson really did drink too much. But he had to be a good man; otherwise

1

he wouldn't have been assigned to this case.

Longarm lifted the newspaper again and rattled it a little as he turned a page. Across the lobby, Harrelson joined in the raucous laughter of the men with him, who actually were traveling salesmen of various stripes.

From the corner of his eye, Longarm looked through the big plate-glass front window of the hotel and saw the two men sitting on the porch. Saw the backs of their heads, actually, since they were facing the street. They looked like drifting cowhands, but in truth they were lawmen too. Longarm knew their names: Bud Seeley and Horace Truelove. Ol' Horace's handle had brought a smile to Longarm's face when Jim Harrelson had pointed them out to him earlier in the evening. There would be time enough later, after the job that had brought them all here was done, for proper introductions.

It was getting on toward time for Nowlan to make his appearance, Longarm thought.

Longarm wasn't often partnered with other deputies. Chief Marshal Billy Vail knew quite well his top man's preference for working alone. But in a case like this, Vail hadn't been willing to take a chance. Uncle Sam had been after Edward Nowlan for more than a year, and after receiving a tip that the master counterfeiter was in Albuquerque, four deputies, including Longarm, had converged on the city at Vail's orders. The word was that Nowlan had a big operation here in New Mexico.

It was about to be shut down.

Longarm turned another page in the newspaper. He wasn't reading the words printed there. The paper was just a prop so that folks wouldn't think there was anything odd about the way he was lingering here in the hotel lobby. Harrelson had ingratiated himself with the drummers for the same reason. Seeley and Truelove could loiter as long as they wanted on the porch, since people did that all the time. All four of them were ready to move at the appropriate moment.

Longarm hoped that would be damned soon. He was getting tired of waiting.

A footstep on the stairs made him glance over the top of the newspaper. A tall, thin man in a town suit was coming down the stairs. Longarm recognized the man's spindly build, the narrow face, the lank, fair hair under the hat. It was Edward Nowlan, right enough, and from the way he moved briskly across the lobby and out the front door, he was on his way to do some business.

As Nowlan turned right and strode off down the boardwalk, Bud Seeley and Horace Truelove stood up, stretched casually, and sauntered in the same direction. A few moments later, Jim Harrelson made his excuses to his new-found cronies and left the lobby as well, pausing just outside the door of the hotel to light a cigar before moving on. Longarm saw the signal over the top edge of the newspaper.

He waited a couple of minutes, then closed and folded the paper, leaving it on the overstuffed armchair as he stood up and straightened the brim of his snuff-brown Stetson. His hand went underneath his coat to his vest pocket and brought out a slim, black cheroot. Without lighting it, he put the cheroot in his mouth and went over to the desk.

The clerk on duty, a young man with pomaded hair, hadn't paid any attention to the comings and goings in the lobby. He was absorbed instead in a yellow-backed dime novel, but he looked up when Longarm cleared his throat.

"Where's the best place to get a drink around here, old son?" asked Longarm.

"Well, the closest place is the Paris Saloon, just down the street," the desk clerk said.

"I asked for the best place, not the closest."

"Why, the Paris is just fine, mister. You won't find colder beer or better whiskey in Albuquerque."

Longarm wondered just how much the proprietor of the Paris Saloon paid the clerk to steer customers his way. Probably not much, maybe just a free drink now and then. But the question had served its purpose, so Longarm didn't argue. He just nodded, said, "Thanks," and left the hotel lobby.

The street outside still had quite a bit of traffic on it

3

despite the late hour. Wagons and buggies rolled along on the paving stones, riders guided their mounts between the vehicles, and pedestrians strolled on the boardwalks. Albuquerque was a bustling place, located as it was not only on the Rio Grande River but also at the intersection of two major trails, one running north and south, the other east and west. The city was ringed with snow-capped mountains on three sides, giving it a picturesque appearance, but the basin in which it lay trapped the heat and made the coolness of the surrounding peaks that much more appealing by contrast. Longarm had been to Albuquerque many times before and liked the town. He wasn't on a sight-seeing trip tonight, however. He turned to his right, spotted Jim Harrelson loitering underneath a street lamp about four blocks away, and started toward him.

The other deputy must have seen Longarm too, because he resumed his walk along the street. All four of the lawmen were on the trail of Nowlan, one of them sticking close, the other three coming along behind at a distance so they would be less likely to be noticed. A man as cunning as Nowlan might have somebody watching his back.

Nowlan had to be pretty smart, or he wouldn't have been able to avoid capture for as long as he had, Longarm thought. But nearly every crook slipped up sooner or later, and when they did, Longarm or some other star-packer was usually waiting to slap the cuffs on them—or ventilate them, if need be.

Longarm hoped it wouldn't come to that tonight, but he wouldn't be surprised if it did. The counterfeiting gang wasn't likely to come along peaceable-like, Not with a pile of phony money at stake, not to mention the engraving plates, which were even more valuable.

Longarm's strong white teeth clenched on the cheroot as he walked along the street, trailing Harrelson. He caught glimpses of the deputy in the derby hat and checked suit as Harrelson moved in and out of the light coming through the windows of the buildings he passed. Harrelson paused at a corner, then turned right, out of Longarm's sight.

When Longarm reached the same corner, he turned too,

and walked a little faster. He couldn't see Harrelson up ahead. Within a couple of blocks, the street and the board-walk were a lot darker. Now that he was away from the saloons and restaurants, Longarm saw that most of the businesses along here were already closed for the night. He knew he wasn't far from the railroad yards. Large, darkened warehouses began bulking up out of the night around him.

A hand came out of the shadows and touched his arm. Longarm reacted instinctively, pivoting sharply and reaching across his body to snag the walnut grips of the Colt .44 in the cross-draw rig on his left hip. The gun came out smoothly, with the faintest whisper of steel on leather, and Longarm's finger was tense and ready on the trigger.

"Hold it, Long!" a familiar voice whispered urgently from the darkness of a recessed doorway. "It's just us, damn it!"

Longarm took a deep breath and tried not to growl in exasperation. "Blast it, Harrelson," he breathed. "Do you know how close I came to shooting you?"

"Too close. Sorry about that, Long. I just didn't want you blundering in on Nowlan and warning him that we're on to him."

Longarm holstered the .44 and said, "Where is he?"

One of the other men with Harrelson said, "He went into that warehouse right up yonder. I reckon that's where the gang's meetin'." The man stuck out his hand in the gloom. "I'm Bud Seeley."

"Custis Long," said Longarm as he shook hands with the man. It looked like there were going to be introductions after all. "Glad to meet you." He turned to the third man. "You'd be Truelove."

"Yeah, and I don't want to hear any comments about it," the man said in a surly voice.

"Don't reckon I blame you," Longarm said mildly. "Would you rather I call you Horace?"

"Can we get on with this?" Harrelson asked before Truelove could answer Longarm's question. "I'm itching to get my hands on Nowlan."

"Sure. How do you want to do this?" asked Seeley.

Harrelson glanced at Longarm. This was Harrelson's bailiwick, and since all four men were deputy marshals, he should have been in charge. But all of them knew Longarm's reputation as the big skookum he-wolf from Billy Vail's office, and they were willing to defer to him, although it might be grudgingly.

Longarm took the cheroot out of his mouth and said quietly to Harrelson, "You know the ground better than any of the rest of us, Jim. What do you say?"

Harrelson seemed relieved that Longarm wasn't going to try to boss the operation. He said, "There's only one back door out of that place. I figured we'd put one man back there and three in front, and then we'll all come in at the same time."

"They're bound to have some guards out," Truelove said. "What about them?"

"Well, I reckon we'll have to spot 'em and put 'em out of commission."

Longarm knew that was going to be more difficult than it sounded, but it didn't necessarily make the plan a bad one.

Seeley rubbed his jaw in thought, then nodded. "I guess we can do that," he said. "Who takes the back?"

"Any volunteers?" asked Harrelson.

"I'll do it," Longarm said. Coming in from the back would be just as dangerous as busting into the warehouse from the front, so he didn't feel like he was ducking a bad job. If anything, he would be in even more danger than the others, because he wouldn't have anybody to watch his back. He would be on his own.

Of course, that was the way he liked it.

Harrelson nodded. "All right. Long goes in the back, the rest of us take the front. In . . . what, ten minutes?"

"Ought to be enough time," Longarm said. "Where's the back door?"

"Far left-hand corner of the building," Harrelson replied. "You can go down the next alley and get to the lane that runs behind the warehouse."

Longarm nodded. He had already figured out that much,

since the warehouse where Nowlan had gone was on the same side of the street as the doorway where this clandestine meeting was taking place.

"Best check your watch," Harrelson added.

Longarm slipped the turnip out of his vest pocket and opened the case. On the other end of the watch chain was a two-shot, .44-caliber derringer instead of a fob. The little gun had saved Longarm's bacon more times than he liked to think about over his years of service as a deputy marshal. Harrelson was still smoking the cigar, so he leaned closer to Longarm and drew on the tightly rolled cylinder of tobacco, making the tip glow a bright red. By that faint light, Longarm saw that the time was twenty minutes past ten.

"I'll come in at ten-thirty," Longarm said as he snapped the watch closed and put it away.

"Good enough," Harrelson said. "We'll wait until then to make our move. If you run into any guards—and you likely will—dispose of 'em as quiet-like as you can."

No, thought Longarm, *I figured I'd have a brass band playing while I clout the son of a bitch over the head with the butt of my pistol.*

He kept the sarcasm to himself and simply nodded again. Then he slid out of the shadows of the doorway and moved along the boardwalk, staying close to the building. When he reached the alley, he stepped down from the walk and moved into its even deeper shadows.

Longarm kept his left hand on the wall of the next building, using it as a guide in the stygian blackness. His right hand was on the butt of his gun. A part of his brain was counting off the seconds as he catfooted along the alley. By the time he got to six hundred, he needed to be in position by the rear door of the warehouse.

Less than a minute had passed when he reached the lane that ran along behind the warehouses. It was narrow and filthy—what he could see of it in the dim light that came from a quarter-moon and a sprinkling of stars in the heavens overhead. He would have to be careful as he made his way along it, lest he knock over some of the trash that had accumulated back there.

He moved out of the alley mouth and started toward the back of the warehouse. It was two buildings away, and as he drew closer, he paused and listened intently, hoping that if any sentries were around, they would do something to give away their position. The little voice in the back of his head continued counting.

The tally was at two hundred when Longarm suddenly heard a soft cough from up ahead of him somewhere. He listened some more, and heard a faint scuff of feet, saw a subtle shifting in the shadows next to the back of the warehouse.

Would the gang have put more than one guard on the back door? That was the question Longarm had to answer, and he had to do it quickly. The count was at two-fifty.

He slid along the wall, using every bit of skill he had picked up over the years from various red men who had been kind enough to teach a clumsy-footed white man how to walk without making quite as much noise as a silvertip grizzly drunk on fermented berries. As a matter of fact, Longarm wasn't making much sound at all as he approached the warehouse. Even the whisper of his gun coming out of its holster couldn't have been heard more than a foot away.

So the counterfeiter on guard duty back here was more than likely surprised as all hell when Longarm tapped him on the shoulder and said, "Howdy."

The man turned instinctively toward the sound, and as his head came around, the butt of Longarm's .44 came crashing down. The blow dented the crown of the man's hat, which softened the impact a little. Longarm had to hit him again before the man slumped forward into his arms, out cold.

"Five hundred," Longarm said aloud. He was there with more than a minute and a half to spare.

That was when all hell broke loose inside the warehouse.

At the sound of the first gunshot, Longarm said, "Shit!" dropped the unconscious gent he had been lowering to the ground, and drove the heel of his boot into the door just below the lock. The wood around it splintered, but it took

8

another kick before the door sprang open and hit the inside wall with a bang.

Longarm went through the opening fast, in a crouching run. There was a short, narrow corridor inside, with another door at the end of it. One kick was enough to open that one, and then he was in the warehouse proper, a huge room with a ceiling two stories high. There were stacks of crates around the walls, and more crates had been used to form partitions in the room, creating several smaller areas. Gunshots and shouted curses came from behind some of those crates. The bullets and the profanity weren't directed at Longarm, however, but rather at the front of the building, where Harrelson, Seeley, and Truelove had found some dubious shelter behind a pair of desks. They were returning the fire.

Despite the fact that he was in a better position than his fellow deputies, Longarm didn't have a clear shot at any of the men behind the crates. The sound of their shots seemed to have drowned out the noise he'd made busting into the place, because no one was shooting at him yet. He went to his left, hoping to get behind the gang before he was spotted.

So far there had been no time to worry about why the raid had been launched early, and that trend continued. Longarm heard a yell of alarm, and one of the pistol barrels behind the crates swiveled toward him. He threw himself to the side as death winked orange from the muzzle of the gun.

Longarm's left shoulder landed hard on the sawdust-littered floor, sending pain shooting through him. He bit back a curse and scrambled behind another stack of crates, snapping a shot toward the gang as he did so. When he reached the shelter of the big wooden boxes, he knelt there and tried to catch his breath.

This place was like a damned maze, he saw now as he looked around. Paths twisted and turned between the stacks of crates, and the handful of lanterns that were lit didn't provide enough light. There were shadows everywhere. Things had probably been set up that way on purpose,

Longarm thought. Anybody who looked inside the warehouse from the street would be unable to see the printing press set up in the center of the big room.

But Longarm had gotten a glimpse of it, and he knew it would be important to the counterfeiters because the plates were probably still locked into it. He had to hope they were, anyway, because while he couldn't get a clear shot at any of the gang from where he was, he thought he might be able to put some slugs into the press.

He sprawled on the floor and edged his head past the corner of the crate. Through a narrow opening, he caught a glimpse of the heavy metal contraption that spewed out the false currency. He triggered three times, fast, and was rewarded by the clang of a bullet striking the press.

"No!" someone cried. That was probably Nowlan, Longarm thought. "Somebody stop him before he ruins everything!"

That was obliging of the fella. Longarm was sure now the plates were still in the press. He sent the final shot in his .44 toward the narrow gap, and then hunkered behind the crates again as bullets chewed bites from the wood and searched like angry hornets through the air around him. He took a box of cartridges from his coat pocket and calmly reloaded the .44. At least, he tried to stay calm. He was sweating again. Damn New Mexico heat.

Longarm could tell from the sound of the shots that Harrelson, Seeley, and Truelove had renewed their attack. Some of the pressure was off them now that more members of the gang were concentrating their fire on Longarm's hiding place. In fact, after a moment the fusillade from the other lawmen increased even more.

That, in turn, took some of the heat off Longarm, and he was able to stand up without worrying too much about getting a bullet through the head. He peeked around the crates and saw how the stacks were lined up. The aisles between them were narrow, so narrow in places that a broad-shouldered man—like Custis Long—might have had to turn sideways to get through them.

He holstered his gun as a plan formed in his mind. Placing his hands against the top crate and flattening his body against the lower boxes in the stack, he started to push.

He wasn't sure what was inside the crates. Considering what was going on in this warehouse, bundles of phony money were the most likely possibility. Whatever was inside the crates, they were heavy enough so that Longarm had to grunt and strain for a long moment before the stack began to tilt.

But when the crates fell, they fell hard, and they landed on more crates, knocking *them* over, and then those crates fell on others. . . .

It was just like little kids playing with dominos, Longarm thought as he stepped back hurriedly and drew his gun again. The falling of the crates continued toward the center of the warehouse, where the gang was holed up. The crashing grew so loud it was deafening.

Dust rose along with the startled shouts of the gang, clogging the air so that it was hard to see. The counterfeiters broke out of hiding abruptly, going all directions at once. Longarm spotted a couple of them coming toward him, guns in their hands.

"Throw down those pistols!" Longarm bellowed. "This is the law!"

The counterfeiters ignored the order and jerked their guns upward.

That was exactly the reaction Longarm had expected. His .44 was already leveled, and he fired twice before either of the men could get off a shot. The slugs bored into their chests, throwing them back so that they disappeared into the clouds of dust again.

The next man came shooting, and Longarm had to dive forward onto his belly. He triggered once as bullets whined over his head. The counterfeiter spun around and tumbled off his feet.

"There goes Nowlan!" a voice shouted urgently. Longarm recognized it as Jim Harrelson's.

The deputies' orders were to take Edward Nowlan alive if possible. A quick death wasn't punishment enough for a man who had made the federal government look like a pack of monkeys for more than a year. The powers that be wanted him behind bars where he could suffer properly. Besides, the theory was that despite being a master engraver, Nowlan wasn't the head of this operation. Someone had backed him. The law wanted to know who.

But sometimes wanting to take a prisoner alive was one thing, and being able to do it was something else entirely. In this case, as Longarm scrambled quickly to his right to intercept the fleeing Edward Nowlan, the counterfeiter pointed the gun in his hand at the deputy and started blazing away.

Nowlan was no gunfighter. None of the bullets struck Longarm. But one of them came close enough to take a hunk out of the brim of his hat, and another practically kissed his ear as it whipped by. Longarm's instincts made him return the fire. He aimed low, however, hoping to cripple Nowlan without mortally wounding him.

That might have been possible if Nowlan's feet hadn't slid on the sawdust on the floor. His legs went out from under him, and he fell as Longarm triggered twice. The first bullet missed, but the second one entered Nowlan's mouth as the man yelped in alarm. The slug tore through Nowlan's throat and out the back of his head, taking the lower third of his brain with it. He was dead, his limbs jerking crazily, by the time he landed on the floor.

"Hell!" Longarm said fervently.

The shots were dying away, and they came to a stop as Longarm strode angrily toward Nowlan's body. "Long!" Harrelson shouted. "Are you all right, Long?"

"Over here," Longarm called in return. "I got Nowlan."

The dust was settling, and Longarm saw Harrelson's bulky shape coming toward him through the thinning clouds. Harrelson stopped beside Nowlan's body and looked down at the corpse with a frown. "We were supposed to take him alive," he said.

"We were supposed to hit the front and back at the same time too," snapped Longarm. "What happened?"

Harrelson's shoulders rose and fell in a shrug. "We made

more noise taking care of the guards out front than I intended. Figured we had already tipped off anybody inside that something was happening, so we decided to get on in here while we could.''

That was reasonable enough, Longarm supposed, although he thought that after warning him to be quiet, Harrelson should have taken a little more care himself. Still, what was done was done, and the dead would stay dead.

There had been seven men in the warehouse besides Nowlan, and five of them had been killed in the fighting. The other two were badly wounded but might live. Truelove was sent outside to check on the unconscious guards. Bud Seeley had caught a slug in the fleshy part of his right arm, but the wound wasn't serious. Harrelson reported this to Longarm as the rangy deputy from Denver knelt next to Nowlan's body.

''I don't reckon we'll get anything really useful from the ones still alive,'' Harrelson went on. ''They're just flunkies. Nowlan ran things. You finding anything?''

Longarm was going through Nowlan's pockets. He pulled out a cheap watch, a handful of coins, a receipt from a Chinese laundry, a ticket to a horse race, and a wallet bulging with folded bills. Longarm slid the money out part of the way and riffled the edges of the bills.

''Queer, more than likely,'' Harrelson said as he looked down at the money.

''No, I think it's the real thing,'' Longarm said. ''From everything we've been told, Nowlan didn't pass the stuff. He just printed it.''

''Well, we'll let somebody else sort it out.''

Longarm tucked Nowlan's wallet back into the dead man's coat and stood up. His long-legged stride carried him through the rubble of the fallen crates toward the printing press, which appeared to be unharmed except for a silver streak on one side of it that had probably been left by Longarm's bullet ricocheting off it.

This wasn't the first counterfeiting operation Longarm had helped bust up. He knew how to take the plates from the press, and within minutes, he had removed them and wrapped them up in a piece of paper torn from a massive roll of the stuff, so that he wouldn't get ink all over his hands. He hefted the little package, which was heavy for its size, and said, "These'll have to go back to Denver."

Harrelson nodded. "Damn right. We can post guards over what's in these crates until somebody figures out what to do with so much phony money, but those plates ought to be with us at all times."

Horace Truelove had come up in time to hear the last comment. He said, "The next train back to Denver isn't until tomorrow evening. What'll we do until then?"

Longarm looked down at the paper-wrapped bundle in his hand and grinned humorlessly. "Looks like we're going to be doing some baby-sitting, boys," he said.

Chapter 2

The Albuquerque police had been told of the planned raid, so when they arrived at the warehouse a few minutes later in response to reports of gunfire, they were prepared for what they found. The guards outside had managed to run off during the shootout, but the two wounded counterfeiters remaining were loaded into a wagon and taken to the hospital, where some of the local star-packers would stand guard over them. The bodies were carted off to the undertaker's. Bud Seeley's arm wound had already been roughly bandaged by Horace Truelove, and the two deputies departed to seek out a doctor who could take a look at the injury. That left Longarm and Jim Harrelson to protect the plates.

Longarm didn't say anything to the police about those valuable little items. He already had them stowed away in a small valise he had found underneath one of the desks where the other deputies had taken cover during the shootout. It wasn't that Longarm didn't trust the local authorities; he just didn't want to place any temptation in their way.

Those plates would be worth a fortune to the right people. They were literally a license to print money.

Despite the weariness that gripped him as midnight came and went, Longarm knew that the counterfeit bills in the crates had to be counted. He and Harrelson and a police captain named Bishop worked on that chore until two o'clock in the morning. When they were finished, Harrelson sighed and shook his head. "Nearly two million dollars worth of the stuff," he said. "Damn, this is some haul!"

"You can count on us to protect it," Captain Bishop declared. "I'll assign my best men to the job."

"You do that, Captain," Longarm said dryly. "Just make sure none of 'em have sticky fingers."

Bishop gave him a cool stare. "If I didn't know you were just doing your job, Marshal, I might be offended by that statement."

"No offense meant," Longarm assured him. He hefted the valise containing the printing plates. "I reckon Marshal Harrelson and I will be going back to the hotel now."

Bishop gestured at the valise. "Do you mind telling me what's in there?"

"Evidence," Harrelson answered curtly. "This is federal business, Captain, not local."

This time Bishop *was* offended, and he didn't bother hiding it. But he didn't ask any more questions, and Longarm and Harrelson were able to leave the warehouse and head back to the hotel.

Longarm lit a cheroot and took a deep draw on it as he and Harrelson walked back to the main street. Harrelson said, "I don't know about you, Long, but I could use a drink."

"Some Maryland rye would go down mighty nice right about now," Longarm agreed, "but I reckon we'd better keep our heads clear until we get back to Denver and turn those plates over to Billy Vail."

"I suppose you're right." Harrelson didn't sound completely convinced, though, and Longarm suspected the man would sneak a swig or two from the flask he carried as soon as he got the chance. Longarm hoped that wasn't going to cause a problem before he got the plates back to Denver.

He blew out a cloud of smoke and said, "We'd better stay in the same room tonight, but don't worry, old son. I ain't getting sweet on you."

Harrelson let out a bark of laughter. "I didn't figure you were. You don't want to leave one man alone with those plates, do you, Long?"

"I trust you, Jim," Longarm said, "and I damn sure trust myself. But I think we'll both be more trustworthy when we're together. Same goes for Bud and Horace."

"Yeah, you're right," Harrelson said with a nod. "Losing two million has got to hurt, but with those plates and a printing press, a fella could have that much again and more in a matter of a few days." He let out a low whistle. "Most men would say a chance like that was worth almost anything. It'd even be worth killing for."

That was what Longarm was afraid of.

The peskiest thing in the world, Longarm thought the next morning, was to have something buzzing around in the back of your head, an idea that wouldn't quite come into focus, yet persisted in prodding your brain.

It was just because he was tired, he told himself. After going on the raid and then staying up all night to guard the plates with Jim Harrelson, he was naturally groggy. That was the reason he kept thinking he had seen *something* the night before that wasn't quite right.

When he and Harrelson got back to the hotel, they had arranged for Seeley and Truelove to have the connecting room next to theirs, so when morning came, Longarm carried the valise into that room and dumped it on the dresser. "There you go, boys," he said to the two deputies, who were just getting up. "You can keep an eye on this while Jim and me get some sleep."

"When does that northbound come through here?" asked Seeley, whose wounded arm bore a more professional bandage now.

"Five o'clock, if my recollection of the schedule is right," Longarm replied.

17

"I'll be glad to be on it and headed back to Denver," Truelove said.

"You and me both," Longarm said. With a wave, he went back through the connecting door. Harrelson was already snoring from his side of the bed. Longarm had never cared for having to share a bunk with another fella, but he was too worn out to be real particular at the moment. He took off his boots, vest, and gunbelt and crawled between the sheets. He was asleep a minute after his head hit the pillow.

"A horse race?" Harrelson said with a frown. "You're going to a horse race?"

It was early afternoon, and Longarm had slept for six hours, long enough to refresh him without leaving him groggy. He was standing in front of the mirror above the room's dressing table, adjusting the string tie around his neck. Harrelson was still in bed, sitting up with his graying hair sticking up in spikes from sleep.

"Don't worry, Jim, I'll be back in plenty of time to catch that train," Longarm said. "I just can't pass up a good horse race."

Harrelson grunted. "Want to get a bet down on one of the nags, is that it?"

"Nope. I just like to see the ponies run." Longarm shrugged into his coat and picked up his hat. He stepped over to the bed and clapped a hand on Harrelson's shoulder. "See you later, Jim. Why don't you step over next door with Bud and Horace while I'm gone, help 'em keep an eye on those plates?"

"Yeah, I reckon that's what I'll do," Harrelson said sourly. "While you're off enjoying yourself," he added.

Longarm just grinned. "Get yourself something to eat first. I did."

In fact, it had been while he was sitting in the hotel dining room downstairs that he had picked up a newspaper and read about the race being held this afternoon at Albuquerque's spanking-new track. Horses from all over, even from as far away as Kentucky, had been brought in for this event. Albuquerque was now part of the western racing circuit, along with El Paso, Tucson, Carson City, Reno, Cheyenne, and Denver. According to the article Longarm read while waiting for the food he had ordered, the horses and their owners and trainers would spend the summer traveling from city to city, taking part in races at each stop. It all sounded pretty interesting to Longarm, and he was going to take in the race in Albuquerque while he had the chance.

He left Harrelson in the hotel room and went back downstairs. One of the porters in the lobby told him where to find the race track and also where he could rent a buggy, since the track was out on the western edge of town, too far to walk.

By the time Longarm reached the racetrack, quite a few people were already there. Buggies and more elaborate carriages were parked in the field next to the track, along with buckboards and ranch wagons. Saddle horses were tied to long hitch racks. Obviously, this race was drawing spectators not only from town but also from most of the ranches in the surrounding area. Some of the spreads were so far out that the families who lived there had probably started into Albuquerque the day before.

Longarm found a place to park the rented buggy and tied the horse to a post. He could see the grandstands on both sides of the track, and they were quickly filling up. He was glad he hadn't waited until later to come out here. The race had generated a lot of interest, and it was clear the stands were going to be full. Longarm lit a cheroot and let his long legs carry him toward the closest grandstand.

He gave his ticket to a fellow in a little building next to the gate and strolled inside with the rest of the crowd. Just as he had thought, there was a wide variety of folks in attendance. He saw townies in store-bought suits and their ladies in fine gowns that had to be stifling hot under the blistering sun, as well as cowboys in range clothes and wide-brimmed Stetsons. Ranchers and their wives, in their Sunday-go-to-meeting best, rubbed shoulders with fancy-suited dudes who were most likely professional gamblers. That was one of the things Longarm liked about any sizable gathering here on the frontier. You were liable to see just about every kind of people there was.

He wasn't prepared, however, for the two individuals who caught his eye as he found a seat and settled down onto the bench.

Two young women were walking along the concourse between the stands and the track. One wore a riding skirt, an open-throated man's shirt, and a flat-crowned brown hat with waves of blond hair sweeping out from under it. The other was attired in a sky-blue gown with a tiny, matching hat perched on an elaborate upsweep of blond curls. The differences between them began and ended with their clothes. Other than that, they seemed to be identical.

For an instant, Longarm wondered if the strain of the past twenty-four hours had him seeing double. Even at a distance, he could tell that there wasn't a dime's worth of difference between the lovely features of the two young women. Even their figures, slender but amply curved in the right places, were the same. Identical twins, Longarm thought. That wasn't something you saw every day.

And you sure as hell didn't run into twins as beautiful as these two very often.

Longarm watched as the two women went over to one of the horses that had been brought out in preparation for the race. A rider in a bright red shirt and tight white pants was on the animal's back, controlling it with a taut rein as it tried to prance around nervously. The blonde in the riding skirt came up to the horse and patted it on the shoulder as she spoke directly to it, rather than to the rider. The horse calmed down a little. It was clear to Longarm from what he observed that the horse was very familiar with the young woman.

The other twin was talking to the rider, evidently either offering encouragement or issuing commands, judging from the way the man kept nodding his head. Longarm couldn't help but wonder about the two young women. What was their connection with a fine-looking chestnut racehorse?

Such speculation wasn't what had brought him here to-day, of course. Maybe when the race was over, he would wander down to the paddock and introduce himself to the ladies, he decided.

"Marshal Long? Is that you?"

The man's voice calling his name so unexpectedly made Longarm look around in surprise. He saw a tall, broad-shouldered man approaching him through the grandstand, trailed by a smaller individual. The man who had called out was rather beefy and florid-faced, with graying dark hair under an expensive felt hat. He wore a dark gray suit. Longarm recognized him right away and stood up to shake the hand the man extended toward him.

"Good to see you again, Senator Padgett," Longarm greeted the man. "What brings you down here?"

Senator Miles Padgett, the junior senator from the great state of Colorado, grinned and said, "I could ask the same thing of you, Marshal, except that I doubt you'd answer me. Billy Vail's probably got you assigned to some secret mission, hasn't he?"

The politician's guess hit a little too close to home, but Longarm didn't reveal that by his expression as he chuckled and said, "No, I'm just here to take in a horse race."

"So am I," said Padgett. "I daresay I've got a slightly bigger stake in the outcome than you do, however. That's my horse down there." He waved toward a rangy blood bay that was being walked back and forth beside the track by its rider.

Longarm quirked an eyebrow, then nodded. "Didn't know you owned a racehorse, Senator."

"It's a recent investment," Padgett explained. "In fact, this will be the first race he's run since I bought him. Why don't you come down to my box and watch the race with us? You'll get a better view than you will up here."

"Thanks," Longarm said with a smile. "Don't mind if I do."

"I'm glad I spotted you," Padgett said as he began to lead the way down to the reserved boxes closer to the track. As an afterthought, he indicated the man with him and said, "You remember Leon Mercer, don't you?"

"Sure," Longarm said with a friendly nod to the man,

who was rather nondescript in a tan suit and brown derby. Longarm recalled that Mercer was just about bald under that derby, despite the fact that he was only about forty. Mercer had been Padgett's assistant and secretary for as long as Longarm had known the senator.

As much as Longarm was around the Federal Building in Denver, it was inevitable that he would make the acquaintance of various politicians, and Miles Padgett was one of them. As a rule, Longarm didn't care much for such gents, but Padgett wasn't bad for somebody who spent so much time in Washington. He was a little pompous and a bit of a glad-hander, but what politico wasn't?

Congress had recessed for the summer, Longarm recalled, and he supposed that was why Padgett was back here in the West. For the sound of it, the senator had bought his way into the racing circuit.

Which meant that he might know who those twin blond lovelies were, Longarm mused. . . .

He and Padgett and Leon Mercer settled themselves down in the seats in the senator's box, and Longarm had to admit that not only was the view much better, the seats were more comfortable than a grandstand bench. He looked for the twins and didn't see them on the concourse; then, as he craned his neck to check out the other boxes, he spotted them sitting nearby. They were alone in their box, although plenty of the male spectators were paying more attention to them than to the horses on the track being brought to the starting line.

The race was about to get underway, so Longarm puffed on his cheroot and turned his eyes back toward the track. The grandstands had been loud with talk and laughter and the music from a brass band at the far end of the track, but now a comparative silence settled down and an air of tense anticipation gripped the crowd. The horses were ready at the starting line, and the starter, a man in a frock coat and top hat, climbed onto a small platform next to the track. He lifted a pistol in his right hand and called out a warning to the riders, letting them know that the race was about to start. A moment later, the pistol cracked as its blank load was fired, and the horses surged forward, galloping for all they were worth.

Senator Padgett came to his feet, and in a voice that had set the walls of Congress to ringing on more than one occasion bellowed, "Come on, Caesar, come on!"

Longarm stood up too. That was the only way to see what was going on. Despite his lack of any real interest in the outcome of the race, he found himself leaning forward, caught up in the emotions running through the crowd. Padgett continued shouting encouragement to his horse, and even his assistant, Leon Mercer, looked excited. Longarm couldn't ever recall seeing anything except a bland, placid expression on Mercer's face. There was something compelling about a horse race, Longarm supposed, that just couldn't be denied.

He took his eyes off the horses long enough to glance over at the box where the two young women were sitting. Of course, they weren't actually sitting anymore. They were standing like everybody else. In fact, they were bouncing up and down in excitement, and Longarm noted with appreciation the effect that motion had on the bosom of the twin wearing the man's shirt. Evidently there wasn't much under that shirt except female flesh, and her breasts were bobbing around invitingly. Once again, Longarm wondered if he could wangle an introduction to them from the senator.

"Run, you bastard, run!" Padgett urged his horse at the top of his lungs. Longarm turned his attention back to the galloping animals and saw that Padgett's blood bay was near the center of the pack. So was the chestnut that the twins had taken an interest in earlier. Neither horse appeared about to make a move to break out of the bunch, but on the other hand, they weren't falling back either.

Longarm leaned over to Padgett and raised his voice to ask, "How long is this race, Senator?"

"A mile and a half!" Padgett replied without taking his eyes off the horses. "Three times around the track!"

The horses had already been around once, and they were nearing the starting line for the second time. As they flashed across in front of the grandstand, Longarm thought that the

23

next time they came back to where they had started, it would be the finish line. He followed the progress of the animals as they swept around the course. The pounding of hooves blended with the shouts of the crowd in a powerful, primitive rhythm. Longarm felt his own pulse speeding up. It was difficult, if not impossible, to keep the enthusiasm of the situation from sweeping him along.

The noise of the crowd grew louder and louder as the horses came toward the finish line, until it was as deafening as the thunder of a thousand storms. The chestnut stallion made a move at the last minute, just enough to break him out of the pack and bring him up into third place as the horses bolted across the line. Senator Padgett's blood bay finished sixth, as far as Longarm could tell. The chestnut's showing was good enough to make the twin blondes jump up and down even harder as they clutched each other in excitement. Padgett just looked mildly disappointed.

"I'm sure Caesar will do better next time, Senator," Mercer said.

"Thank you, Leon. I certainly hope so." Padgett turned to Longarm. "And I hope you didn't have any money down on my horse, Marshal."

Longarm shook his head. "As far as I'm concerned, Senator, this was just an exhibition, not a competition. I didn't do any wagering."

"Well, I did," muttered Padgett. "I didn't lose my shirt, though." He started out of the box. "Come on. I suppose I should go congratulate the winning owner, and then I want to buy you a drink, Marshal."

That sounded all right to Longarm, so he followed Padgett out of the box. Mercer came along too, of course. The three men made their way through the crowd to a gate that led down to the concourse. They reached the opening at the same time as the two young women who looked so much alike.

That was a stroke of luck, Longarm thought. Padgett tipped his hat and stepped back so that the women could precede him. "After you, ladies," he said gallantly.

The one in the sky-blue dress smiled at him, dimpling

prettily. "Why, thank you, Senator," she said, her voice lightly touched with a honey-sweet Southern drawl.

"Come on, Janice," the other twin said, her tones crisper and more businesslike. "I want to see how Matador is doing."

Longarm had doffed his hat too. The young woman called Janice looked over at him and smiled as she followed her sister down the steps to the concourse. Longarm returned the smile, then put his hat on again and stepped up next to Padgett. "Those are mighty nice-looking young ladies," he said to the politician. "You know 'em?"

"You mean the Cassidy sisters?" asked Padgett. "Indeed I do. Not well, of course, since we only met recently. They own that chestnut horse that finished third, the one Miss Julie called Matador."

That came as something of a surprise to Longarm. He had figured the chestnut was owned by the father of the young women, or perhaps by the husband or gentleman friend of one of them.

"Miss Julie trained the horse herself," Padgett went on. "They have a horse breeding farm in Missouri, I believe. Very exceptional young ladies."

"I reckon so," Longarm said.

Padgett grinned. "And as you noticed, quite striking as well, and both unmarried. I'll introduce you to them."

That was exactly what Longarm wanted. He nodded to the senator and said, "Thanks. I'd like that."

Padgett led the way down onto the concourse and over to the spot where the blood bay was blowing heavily. The horse's rider, who wore a green shirt and white pants, had already slipped down from the saddle and was stroking the bay's flanks. The young man looked back over his shoulder nervously as he saw Padgett coming.

"I'm sorry, Senator," he said quickly before Padgett could say anything. "I did the best I could. We were just packed in there too tight."

"I understand, Cy," Padgett said. "Don't worry about it. You did fine."

The rider looked surprised. "Are you sure? I mean, I

know how much you wanted to win, Senator.''

Padgett answered with a casual wave of a hand. ''Don't give it another thought. Just ride a good race next time.''

Cy bobbed his head. ''Yes, sir. I sure will, you can count on that.''

Longarm wondered if the boy was in for a bawling out later in private. Cy had certainly looked like he expected Padgett to be angry with him for not winning. Longarm recalled that Padgett had been elected to the Senate on his first run at public office, and he had successfully staved off every challenger since then. Padgett was a man accustomed to winning, and winning big. Losing even something like a horse race probably galled him.

Padgett turned to Longarm and said, ''Come along, Marshal. I want you to meet the Cassidy sisters now.''

Longarm wanted that too, so he followed Padgett without complaint. They strode over to the spot where the two blondes were still fussing over their horse.

''Congratulations, ladies,'' Padgett said to them. ''Matador ran a gallant race.''

''He should have won,'' Julie Cassidy said.

''Perhaps next time he will,'' Janice added. Again she smiled at Longarm. ''Who's your handsome friend, Senator?''

Padgett chuckled. ''I brought him over here to introduce him to you, but perhaps I shouldn't, Miss Janice. You never flirt with *me* like that.''

Janice Cassidy turned her dazzling smile on him. ''Why, I do so!'' she said as she lifted a gloved hand to the senator's cheek. ''I flirt shamelessly with you every time I see you, you old dear.''

Padgett basked in the glow of her attention for a second, then somewhat grudgingly said, ''This is Custis Long. He's a United States deputy marshal from the Denver office.''

''A deputy marshal!'' Janice exclaimed. ''How exciting.''

''It's just another job, ma'am,'' Longarm told her as he took the hand she extended to him. He wasn't sure if he was supposed to kiss the back of it or not, but since he didn't often go in for such fancy greetings, he just shook it instead.

There was no question that was what Julie Cassidy expected. She shook hands forthrightly, like a man, and her grip was strong and firm. "Pleased to meet you, Marshal," she said.

Julie turned back to the chestnut stallion and issued orders for him to be taken back to the paddock and rubbed down properly. In the meantime, Janice sidled closer to Longarm and linked her arm with his without being invited to do so. "I know I'm being quite bold, Marshal," she said, "but would you like to have a drink with us in the clubhouse? I believe Matador's strong finish calls for some champagne."

Longarm had never cared much for French bubbly water, but he wasn't in the habit of turning down invitations from women as beautiful—and friendly—as Janice Cassidy. "I'd be pleased and honored to join you, ma'am," he said.

"Come along then." Janice looked over at Padgett. "You'll join us too, won't you, Senator?"

"Of course," replied Padgett. "You're a lucky man, Marshal. Miss Janice seems to have taken a shine to you."

"Go on with you!" Janice said to him. "Why, Marshal Long and I are just friends. Isn't that right, Marshal?"

"Whatever you say, ma'am." Longarm hoped the grin on his face didn't look too self-satisfied. Janice was overdoing the flirtatiousness, of course, but that seemed to be her personality. He certainly wasn't going to tell her to stop.

They started strolling toward the clubhouse at the other end of the grandstands. Senator Padgett and Julie Cassidy followed behind them, trailed by Leon Mercer. Janice leaned her head closer to Longarm's and asked in a low voice so that the others couldn't overhear, "Did Senator Padgett tell you my sister and I have a horse farm in Missouri?"

"Yes, ma'am, I believe he mentioned that," Longarm replied.

"Well, you're going to have to visit us there sometime, Marshal. We'd love to have you." Janice's voice became

27

even huskier as she went on. "You see, my sister and I do *everything* together, if you know what I mean, even entertaining company. I'm sure you'd never forget a visit to our place."

There was no mistaking the meaning in her voice and in her eyes. Longarm had to swallow hard before he could say, "No, ma'am, I don't imagine I would."

He wasn't sure what he had expected to find at the racetrack today . . . but the Cassidy sisters certainly weren't it!

Chapter 3

Jim Harrelson lifted the flask to his lips and took a long swig of the whiskey inside it. The liquor made his insides glow warmly all the way down, and then lit a fire in his belly.

Damn Custis Long anyway.

Longarm was a good lawman, there was no doubt about that. If he hadn't been along on that raid the night before, Nowlan might have gotten away. Those oh-so-valuable printing plates might not have been recovered. But that didn't give Longarm any right to act like he was the chief marshal or something, giving orders about no drinking. He was just a badge-toter for Uncle Sam, like the rest of them.

Harrelson capped the flask, stowed it away inside his coat, and stepped out of the little room down the hall from the room where Bud Seeley and Horace Truelove were playing cards as they stood guard over the plates. This hotel was the only one in Albuquerque with that newfangled indoor plumbing, and Harrelson was thankful for it. Stepping just down the hall for a quick trip was a lot easier than having to pay a visit to the outhouse behind the hotel. Smelled better too.

29

Bud and Horace probably thought he had the trots, he told himself with a chuckle as he walked down the deserted hall, his steps only a trifle unsteady. He had gone down the hall quite a few times this afternoon.

But he had a right! Hell, Longarm had ducked out and gone to a horse race, of all things! If Longarm was out enjoying himself, then there was nothing wrong with him having a drink or two—or six—Harrelson thought.

A man appeared at the far end of the second-floor corridor, at the head of the staircase. Harrelson didn't pay much attention to him, even though the man started along the hallway toward him. They were going to pass each other just before Harrelson reached the door to the room shared by the other two deputies.

The man stopped, however, and asked, "Do you know where Room Seven is, pard?"

Harrelson still only glanced at the gent, seeing a man in well-kept range clothes. The lawman half-turned and gestured with his thumb toward a door down the hall. "Down there," he grunted.

Suddenly, before he could turn back, an arm shot around his neck and a hand on his shoulder gave him a rough shove. He was jerked around so that the man who had stopped him was behind him. Harrelson tried to open his mouth to yell, but an inexorable pressure forced his chin up, keeping his lips closed and drawing his neck tight. Something that was cold and hot at the same time slid across the front of his throat. A warm, sticky flood splashed onto his chest, and he heard a horrible gurgling sound that he knew somehow was coming from him, even though his mouth was still closed.

Those were the last things Jim Harrelson ever knew. He was dead before the man who had just killed him had time to lower his body to the carpet runner in the center of the hall. Within seconds, that carpet had quite a bloodstain on it.

The killer stepped diagonally across the hall to another door and rapped softly on it. The door was opened, and the man inside looked out calmly at the carnage in the corridor.

He nodded, made a motion with his hand, and he and several other men hurried out of the room.

It was the middle of the afternoon, and the hotel was hot and quiet as the stifling heat of the day built up.

"Beat that," Bud Seeley said as he laid his cards down on the table inside the hotel room. Horace Truelove looked glumly at the full house, jacks over nines, and shook his head as he threw in his own cards.

"Can't," he said simply.

Seeley chuckled as he raked in the pile of matches in the center of the table. "That's thirty-seven thousand dollars you owe me, Horace. Considerin' the wages that Uncle Sam gives us, you ought to be able to pay me off . . . in a hundred years or so."

Truelove lifted his head and turned his face toward the door. A frown creased his brow. "You hear something a minute ago?" he asked.

"Like what?"

Truelove's frown deepened. "I'm not right sure. It was strange, though, I know that."

"Only thing strange around here is the run of luck I'm havin'," said Seeley. He gathered up the deck and started to shuffle. "Here we go again."

A knock sounded on the door.

Both deputies tensed. The door was locked, of course, and if Harrelson had gotten back from the facilities, he wouldn't have knocked. He would have just called out for the two men inside to let him in.

"Could be somebody from the hotel," Seeley suggested.

"Yeah, or Long's got back early." Truelove stood up. "I'll see who it is." He went over to the door, standing carefully to one side as he called out, "Who's there?"

A man's voice asked, "Mister, you got a friend name of Harrelson?"

Truelove glanced at Seeley, who shook his head and shrugged. Neither of them recognized the voice. Truelove turned back to the door and said, "What's it to you?"

"Not a damn thing. But I just came along the hall, and

there's a man out here lying on the floor who's powerful sick. He says his name is Harrelson and that he knows somebody in this room.''

The glance that Truelove directed toward Seeley this time was full of disgust. He didn't believe for a second that Harrelson was really sick. All afternoon, Harrelson had been sneaking off for a drink, and he seemed to actually think that the other two deputies didn't know what he was doing. Seeley grinned coldly and pantomimed a drinking motion. Truelove just nodded. They would have to drag Harrelson in from the hall and try to sober him up, or there might be trouble when Longarm got back.

''Just a minute,'' Truelove said as he took a key from his shirt pocket, thrust it into the door lock, and turned it. As he opened the door, he asked, ''Where is he?''

A ray of sunlight coming through the window at the end of the hallway glittered for a second on polished steel. Truelove saw that, realized what it meant, and reached desperately for the gun on his hip.

He was too late.

''It's getting late,'' said Longarm. ''I'd better head back to the hotel.''

''Late?'' Janice Cassidy echoed as she leaned closer to Longarm. The soft thrust of her breast pressed against his arm. ''Why, it's only the middle of the afternoon!''

Longarm glanced at the clock on the wall of the bar in the racetrack clubhouse. It was a banjo clock, much like the one in Billy Vail's office in the Denver Federal Building. As a rule, they kept good time, and this one said that the hour was rapidly approaching four o'clock.

''Maybe so, ma'am, but I've got a train to catch,'' Longarm explained. ''I have to be on the five o'clock northbound.''

Janice pouted prettily. ''So you'd rather be sitting in some smoky, uncomfortable train car than drinking champagne with me?''

''Not hardly! Can't neglect my duty, though.''

''You men and your duties,'' Janice said disgustedly.

"Don't you ever think about anything else?"

"Oh, yes, ma'am," Longarm replied fervently. "We sure do."

He had been thinking a lot of things during the past hour as he shared a bottle of champagne with the Cassidy sisters and Senator Miles Padgett in the luxuriously appointed clubhouse. The place was all dark wood and low lighting, just the sort of atmosphere to put ideas into a fella's head when he was sitting across a table from an obviously wanton young lovely such as Janice Cassidy.

Julie was not without her own charms either. She was every bit as beautiful as her sister, only more reserved. Still, several times Longarm had noticed her watching him with a strange glow in her eyes, and he couldn't help but recall what Janice had said about the two of them doing everything together.

The image *that* conjured up in his head was enough to make any man perk up.

Unfortunately, Longarm had never been the sort to forget about his other responsibilities. He had to deliver those counterfeiting plates back to Denver, and the Cassidy sisters would be moving on with the racing circuit. The next stop was El Paso, and then the circuit would head west to Arizona. There was a good chance Longarm would never see Janice and Julie again unless fate happened to take him somewhere near their horse farm in Missouri.

At the moment, he was alone at the table with Janice. Julie and Padgett had gone to the bar to get another bottle of champagne. The senator was thoroughly enjoying himself this afternoon. He seemed to have gotten over his disappointment at his horse's showing in the race. Leon Mercer had wandered off somewhere and was probably waiting for Padgett outside.

Although Longarm wouldn't have thought it was possible, Janice moved even closer to him, the legs of her chair scraping a little on the hardwood floor. Her right thigh was pressed warmly against his left leg now. She smiled at him and said, "Well, Custis, if you're so determined to leave,

33

I suppose I'm just going to have to give you something to remember me by.''

Her hand touched his thigh, slid over it into his lap.

He had spent the last hour half-erect to start with from Janice's provocative comments and glances. The touch of her soft, warm fingers, even through the fabric of his trousers, completed the job. His shaft sprang to full, rather uncomfortable attention.

"Wait just a second there, ma'am," Longarm said hurriedly as Janice caressed him. "We're in sort of a public place."

"No one can see what I'm doing under the table," Janice replied sweetly. "It's too dim in here for that. Besides, I don't care." She ran her hand along the length of him and went on. "My goodness, you certainly are an impressive man, Marshal Long!"

"Ma'am—''

"Please don't call me that. I think our friendship has grown much too close for such formality, don't you?''

Considering how enthusiastically she was squeezing his pecker, Longarm supposed she was right.

"Now, where are those buttons . . .'' murmured Janice.

"Ma'am—Janice—you can't be thinking of—''

"Ah, there they are! Now, don't make a scene, Marshal. Just sit still, and I'll take care of everything.''

That was what Longarm was afraid of.

He glanced toward the bar. Senator Padgett and Julie Cassidy were deep in conversation with several men standing there—other horse owners, Longarm guessed. They weren't paying any attention to what was going on at the table they had left. Nor did anyone else in the room seem to be looking in the direction of Longarm and Janice.

She was opening the buttons of his fly with practiced ease. This wasn't the first time she had reached into a fella's pants, Longarm thought. Then he was beyond thinking much of anything as her nimble fingers freed his organ and closed around the throbbing, rock-hard pole of flesh.

Janice's tongue darted out of her mouth and licked over her lips. "Nice, very nice," she whispered in his ear. "I'd dearly love to have that big ol' thing inside me right now, Custis. I suppose we'll just have to make do, though.'' Her palm slid up and down his shaft with maddening slowness.

Longarm tried not to gulp. ''You'd best be careful,'' he managed to say, ''or you're liable to get more than you expect, ma'am. I mean Janice.''

She purred like a cat and said, ''Oh, I expect it, all right. In fact, I crave it, Custis. You just go ahead and give it to me any time you're ready.''

''Lordy!'' he muttered. He had run across some brazen women in his time, but Janice Cassidy took the cake. He couldn't believe what she was doing to him . . . just like he couldn't believe he was letting her do it in the middle of this racetrack clubhouse.

He felt his climax approaching inexorably. Janice must have felt it too, because with her other hand she plucked a lacy handkerchief from the bosom of her dress and got it under the table without any wasted motions. Yep, definitely not the first time she had done this, Longarm decided. He put the palms of his hands on the table and pressed down hard as spasms rippled through him. Janice had the handkerchief in place to catch his seed as it jetted out. Longarm drew a deep, ragged breath as she used the cloth to wipe him clean and squeeze the last of his juice from him. She had sure as hell drained him. A pulse was hammering in his skull, and he was light-headed.

Janice tucked him back into his pants and said with a smile, ''See, I told you you'd remember me.''

''I don't reckon I could ever forget *that*,'' Longarm gasped out.

''Button yourself up discreetly, Custis,'' she said as she put the handkerchief away in her bag.

''Yes, ma'am.'' He was a tiny bit annoyed with her superior attitude. She probably thought that she had him right where she wanted him now. It would be mighty nice, he told himself, to get this sweet little honey onto a soft mattress between some cool sheets and bring her to a screaming, shuddering climax. Maybe one of these days . . .

If not for those damned counterfeiting plates!

He sighed. "I've really got to be going now. I'm sorry, Janice."

"No, that's all right," she told him. "You go ahead and do your duty, Custis. I'm not sure what it is, mind you, but I'm certain it's important."

"It'd have to be," he muttered as he finished fastening his pants. He pushed himself to his feet.

"Remember what I told you about coming to see us."

"Yes, ma'am. I mean Janice."

Senator Padgett turned away from the bar and started toward the table, Julie Cassidy on his arm. They increased their pace a bit when they saw Longarm standing up.

"Leaving us so soon, Marshal?" asked Padgett as he and Julie returned to the table.

"Got to catch a train," Longarm said. He shook hands with Padgett and then smiled and nodded at Julie. "Be seeing you, Miss Julie."

"I hope so," she said, and he caught the undertone of desire in her voice. She might be a lot cooler on the outside than her sister, but Longarm had the feeling that the fires burned just as hot inside.

He gave the senator and the twins a smile and a casual wave and started toward the door of the clubhouse, fishing out a cheroot as he went. His teeth clamped down on the cylinder of tobacco as he stepped out of the cool dimness of the building into the late afternoon heat.

Leon Mercer was walking toward him, pausing every couple of steps to drag his shoe on the ground. The man was frowning darkly and muttering. Longarm grinned as Mercer came up to him. "Step in something, Leon?"

"This is a racetrack, Marshal," Mercer said. "There are horses all over the place. How could one *help* but step in something occasionally?"

"That's mighty true," agreed Longarm. "That's why it pays to watch where you're going."

"Indeed." Mercer gestured at the clubhouse. "Is the senator still inside?"

"Yep."

"Good. Some journalists want to talk to him about the

tariff bill Congress will be considering in the fall. I'll get him.''

"Good luck dragging him away from those Cassidy sisters,'' Longarm said dryly.

For the first time, Longarm saw a faint smile on Mercer's face. "Oh, he'll come along. It's a rare politician who can resist the lure of the press.''

Longarm chuckled and clapped him on the shoulder. "I reckon you're right about that too. So long, Leon.''

He walked quickly back to where he had left the rented buggy as Mercer disappeared into the clubhouse in search of Senator Padgett. The afternoon had been surprising in more ways than one, Longarm thought as he untied the team from the hitching post and stepped up into the buggy. Whether it had been meaningful or not was something he just couldn't say as yet.

He turned the buggy back toward the hotel.

As soon as he stepped into the lobby of the hotel after returning the buggy to the stable, he knew something was wrong.

Damned wrong.

Captain Bishop of the Albuquerque police was standing next to the desk, talking to the clerk on duty. The clerk's face was pale and haggard, and his forehead had a sheen of sweat on it that Longarm sensed had little to do with the heat. The man's eyes widened as he glanced over and saw Longarm coming into the lobby. He raised his arm and pointed at the lawman.

Bishop turned to face him, and the local badge-toter's expression was grim. Longarm frowned as he walked quickly over to the desk. "What's happened?'' he asked.

"I've been wondering where you were, Marshal,'' Bishop said without answering Longarm's question. "Nobody around here seemed to know.''

"I went to the horse race,'' Longarm said. "Anything wrong with that?''

"Did you place any bets?'' asked Bishop.

Longarm's frown deepened. "Didn't feel like it.''

"You should have," Bishop said coolly. "You were obviously running a string of good luck this afternoon. You're still alive, and your friends aren't."

Longarm didn't want to start cussing a fellow lawman in public like this, but he was getting mighty exasperated with Bishop. His jaw taut with anger, he asked, "What happened to them?"

"Come upstairs and see for yourself." Bishop inclined his head toward the staircase on the other side of the lobby.

There were a couple of blue-uniformed officers at the top of the stairs, Longarm saw as he and Bishop started up to the second floor. He noticed now too that the lobby was empty of hotel guests. Clearly, the police had taken the place over and clamped the lid on tight. Worry gnawed on Longarm's brain. Bishop had said that the other three deputy marshals were dead, and Longarm had a pretty good idea what that meant. He didn't expect to find those printing plates upstairs when he got there.

The two policemen stepped aside to let Longarm and Bishop pass. The first thing Longarm noticed as he and the captain started down the hallway was the huge bloodstain on the carpet runner, about halfway down the corridor. Right outside the door of the room where Bud Seeley and Horace Truelove were supposed to be standing guard over the plates, in fact.

Longarm's insides twisted. Nobody lost that much blood and lived to talk about it. There was no corpse in the hallway, though. He said, "Where are they?"

Bishop grunted. "Inside the room. One of the other guests found that pool of blood and ran downstairs screaming. The clerk and one of the porters came up here and found the bodies inside. The clerk used his key to get in when he noticed more blood running out from under the door."

Longarm's face was frozen into a bleak grimace by now. He said, "I reckon they sent for you then."

"The clerk had already sent another porter for the law. We got here a few minutes later." Bishop had reached the door of the marshals' room. He was careful not to step in the blood as he reached for the doorknob. The blood was mostly dry by now, but it would still be sticky. "You ready for this?"

Longarm took a deep breath and wished he hadn't. The sharp, sheared-copper smell of spilled blood filled his nostrils. He managed to nod.

Bishop turned the knob and swung the door back. Through the opening, Longarm saw the bodies sprawled on the floor of the room. He steeled himself and stepped inside.

Jim Harrelson was the closest to the door. His throat had been cut so deeply that his head seemed to be barely hanging on to his shoulders. Horace Truelove was next. He looked like he had been stabbed at least a dozen times in the chest, and his throat was slashed as well. At first glance, Bud Seeley, who lay curled up beside the bed, didn't seem to be injured at all. But then Longarm saw the wound in the side of his neck where a knife had gone in.

"All of them were killed quick and quiet," Bishop said, "by somebody who knew how to use a knife. Looking at it, the blood out in the hall seems to have come from Harrelson. Most of it in here came from Truelove."

"Son of a bitch," Longarm muttered. Nobody deserved to come to an end like this, slaughtered like some sort of animal.

He forced his gaze away from the horrible tableau and looked around the room. There was no sign of the valise which had held the counterfeiting plates. That came as no surprise to him. He stepped over to the dresser, checked quickly through its drawers, then opened the doors of the wardrobe that stood against one wall. The meager traveling gear belonging to the federal lawmen was there, but no valise, no package of any sort that could have contained the plates.

"What are you looking for, Marshal?" Bishop asked sharply. "The 'evidence' you and Harrelson took out of that warehouse early this morning?"

Longarm didn't see any point in keeping it a secret any longer. "The printing plates," he said. "The ones Edward Nowlan used to make that two million in phony currency."

Bishop let out a low whistle. "I thought it might be something like that. Didn't you trust us, Marshal?"

"We were just trying to cut down on the chances of something like this happening," Longarm said with a curt wave at the carnage around them.

Bishop bristled at that comment. "Are you saying you thought my men couldn't be trusted? You think one of them had something to do with this?"

"No offense, Captain, but when something as valuable as those plates is involved, I don't trust *myself* overmuch, let alone anybody else. And I was right to be worried. *Somebody* knew about those plates and had a pretty good idea where to find them."

Without saying anything else, he strode over to the connecting door and opened it, stepping into the room he and Harrelson had shared. Bishop trailed him as he searched the room quickly but thoroughly, not turning up a damned thing.

Longarm sighed. "I thought maybe there was a chance one of the boys had put the plates in here. Didn't think it was very likely, though, and I was sure enough right about that part of it."

Bishop jerked a thumb over his shoulder at the bodies of the federal men. "Now that you've seen everything, is it all right if I get some of my men in here and have those bodies taken out?"

Longarm nodded and said, "Sure. I reckon those poor bastards are long past being able to tell us anything about who did this to 'em."

He lit a fresh cheroot to help cover up the smell of the blood and told himself not to feel guilty because he was alive and Harrelson, Seeley, and Truelove were dead. Going to the horse race had been giving in to an impulse, that was all. He'd had no way of knowing that his fellow lawmen would be murdered while he was gone.

Yet a part of him insisted that he should have been here, should have done something to prevent this massacre. He hadn't known the three dead men very well, but they had all carried a badge. In that sense, they were all his brothers.

Bishop came back from issuing orders to his men and found Longarm smoking gloomily and peering out the window of the hotel room, his back to the corpses. "What are you going to do now, Marshal?" asked the local lawman.

"Don't have much choice," Longarm said without looking around. "I was supposed to catch the five o'clock train for Denver, but there wouldn't be any point to it now. I was supposed to deliver those printing plates to my boss, but they're long gone." He rolled the cheroot from one side of his mouth to the other. "Reckon I'll just have to find 'em—and the sons o' bitches who did this."

"I hope you do," Bishop said quietly.

Longarm sighed and turned away from the window, still not looking at the corpses. "Guess I'd better send a wire to my boss and let him know what happened. I'd sure hate to be Henry in a little while."

"Who's Henry?" Bishop asked with a confused frown.

"The young fella who plays the typewriter in Billy Vail's front office. He's the one who'll have to carry in the telegraph message I'm going to send."

"Oh." Bishop seemed to understand now.

Longarm started toward the door, then paused abruptly. Something on the floor had caught his attention. There were plenty of bloodstains, of course, but this seemed to be some other sort of stain. . . .

The door opened and several burly policemen came into the room carrying canvas tarpaulins. Longarm knew why they were there, and he stepped aside so that they could get started on their grim task of rolling up the bodies in the canvas and carrying them out of here. The next stop for Harrelson, Seeley, and Truelove would be the undertaker's.

Bishop put a hand on Longarm's shoulder. "Come on, Marshal. Let's get out of here."

Longarm nodded. There was nothing more he could do here now. The dead men were far beyond any help he could muster for them.

But as far as vengeance went, once he caught up to the men who had done this . . . well, that was another story entirely. Longarm figured he could handle that just fine.

Chapter 4

Being a lawman wasn't all gunfights with sneering desperados and rescuing beautiful damsels in distress, like those dime novel scribblers back East had it. A lot of the work that went with packing a badge consisted of trudging from place to place and asking the same questions over and over again. That was what Longarm did for the rest of the afternoon. Bishop and the local officers could have probably handled this part of the investigation just fine, and truth to tell, they'd likely cover the same ground whether Longarm did or not, but he felt like he had to give it a try.

He owed the three dead marshals that much.

Not that his legwork did any good. By late that evening, he had talked to all the guests and employees of the hotel, plus everyone he could find in the other businesses along the block. No one had seen or heard anything—or anyone—suspicious coming from the second floor of the hotel that afternoon. The hotel was one of Albuquerque's best, so there were usually quite a few people coming and going. A few more wouldn't be noticed unless there was something odd about them.

Longarm considered that and decided at least one of the

killers must have changed clothes before leaving the hotel. With all the blood that had been spilled, some of it was bound to have splattered on the man or men who had wielded the knife. Plus the killers would have had the valise containing the counterfeiting plates. But who in blazes would find anything strange, or memorable, about several men leaving a hotel and carrying bags? It happened all the time, every day.

Longarm moved to another room, this one on the third floor of the hotel. The murderers had no reason to come back and try for him—they had gotten what they wanted, after all—but it was the sort of precaution he automatically took. That careful nature had kept him alive for a long time in a dangerous business.

As he sprawled out on the bed wearing only the bottom half of a pair of summerweight long underwear and puffing on a cheroot, he thought about everything that had happened in the past twenty-four hours. It had been an eventful period, packed with violence and death. There were moments when Longarm thought he was getting too old and too tired for this sort of life. This was one of those times.

But he sure couldn't go back to cowboying, and he hadn't done much else with his life since drifting out to the frontier from West-by-God Virginia after the Late Unpleasantness had come to a close at Appomattox Courthouse. Packing a badge was all he knew, and he figured he'd keep at it until his luck finally ran out and he died in some dark back alley or dingy hotel room or smoky saloon.

With his mind drifting like that, something tried to prod its way forward in his brain and call attention to itself. He frowned and reached out mentally to grasp it, but it abruptly slid away from him, and no matter what he did, he couldn't quite manage to recall it. Finally, he shook his head in frustration, butted out the cheroot, rolled over, and surprised himself by falling into a deep, dreamless sleep.

There was a message waiting for Longarm when he came downstairs the next morning. The clerk called his name and held up a piece of paper as Longarm started across the lobby.

Longarm went over to the desk, and the man behind it said, "I was about to send a boy up to your room with this, Marshal. It was just delivered a moment ago."

"Thanks." Longarm took the message and dropped a coin onto the counter. The coin disappeared with amazing alacrity. Longarm unfolded the paper and read:

MARSHAL LONG, PLEASE MEET ME AT THE RACETRACK SOMETIME THIS MORNING. YRS TRULY, MILES PADGETT.

Longarm frowned. What did the senator want with him? Although the message had been phrased as a request, Longarm knew it was more in the nature of a command. He sighed, then brightened a little. He had woken up this morning with a nebulous plan in his head, and a visit to the racetrack would fit right in with what he had in mind. In fact, this might work out for the best.

He folded the paper again and slipped it into his vest pocket, then nodded his thanks once more to the clerk before heading for the dining room. He wasn't going to drop everything and rush out to the track just because Padgett had requested his presence. First he wanted some breakfast, and then there were a few more errands he needed to run. He wasn't sure what Padgett wanted, but he planned to cooperate with the senator as much as possible . . . within reason. When you came right down to it, though, Padgett wasn't Longarm's boss, not by any stretch of the imagination.

Three cups of strong coffee, a stack of flapjacks swimming in syrup and melted butter, half a dozen thick strips of bacon, and a mound of scrambled eggs later, Longarm felt almost like a new man.

He left the hotel and headed for the Western Union office.

The senator's rangy blood bay—Caesar, Longarm remembered the horse was called—was loping easily around the

45

track when Longarm arrived. Padgett was leaning against the railing around the track, watching the horse exercise. He turned and lifted a hand in greeting as Longarm called, "Good morning, Senator."

"I'm not so sure about that." Padgett's face was set in a concerned frown. "I heard about the trouble you had at the hotel yesterday."

Longarm grimaced. The story of the murders hadn't been in the newspaper this morning, other than the fact that there had been an unspecified disturbance at the hotel. Bishop had promised to try to keep it quiet, and Longarm had thought the local badge had been successful in that effort.

"Pardon my asking, Senator, but what exactly have you heard?"

"About the murders of your fellow lawmen and the theft of some sort of valuable evidence. I'm not completely clear on that part, but I'm hoping you'll shed some light on the subject."

"How did you hear about it?"

Padgett waved away the question. "I have my sources. Well, Marshal?"

Longarm drew a deep breath that, given the surroundings, inevitably smelled a little like horseshit. He said, "Begging your pardon again, Senator, but I'm afraid it's not any of your damned business."

The politician's cheeks grew even more florid than usual, and for a second Longarm worried that he might have a stroke right then and there. Then Padgett's features relaxed slightly, and a moment later he even chuckled. "Sorry, Marshal," he said. "It's just that I'm not accustomed to being spoken to in that manner. But I must say, I rather admire it. You're right, of course. This matter has to do with official business of the United States marshal's office, not the Senate. I'm pretty much a civilian where you're concerned."

"Well, maybe not quite the same as a civilian," said Longarm. There was no point in going out of his way right now to antagonize the man. "I can tell you that what you heard is pretty much right. Three deputy marshals were killed yesterday afternoon, and all four of us were here in Albuquerque on a case. We were supposed to go back to Denver yesterday, like I said in the clubhouse. Now I'm sort of at loose ends.''

"But you're going to pursue the killers, aren't you?''

Longarm nodded. "I reckon so. I'm waiting for official word from Billy Vail, though.''

"It sounds like a terrible, terrible tragedy,'' Padgett said with a shake of his head. "Did any of the dead men have families?''

Longarm frowned. He didn't know—and that just made him feel worse about the situation. "If they did, Marshal Vail will contact them and break the bad news.''

"Terrible,'' Padgett said again. He sighed. "But life must go on, I suppose.'' He gestured toward the track. "What do you think of Caesar this morning?''

Longarm looked at the horse and saw that it was running smoothly and easily along the track. "Same as yesterday. That's a fine-looking animal you've got there, Senator.''

"I think so too. I have to admit, though, I was certainly disappointed in the outcome of the race. Perhaps we'll do better in El Paso.''

"When are you leaving?'' asked Longarm, thinking of the Cassidy sisters, among other things. It would be nice to see Janice and Julie again. He felt a stirring inside him at the memory of what the brazen Janice had done to him in the clubhouse the day before.

"The southbound train will be here tonight, and we'll get into El Paso first thing in the morning. The race is scheduled for three days from now, so Cy will have time to get himself and Caesar accustomed to the course.'' Padgett nodded toward the track as horse and rider swept by once again. "I wanted Caesar to have a little exercise this morning before he's taken back to the stable and then loaded onto a train car tonight.''

Longarm nodded. "Good idea. Wouldn't want him to stiffen up.''

Padgett turned to rest his arms on the fence as he leaned on it again. "Well, I appreciate you coming out here, Marshal,'' he said as Longarm joined him at the fence. "I just wanted to find out the truth of the rumors I'd heard. Is there anything I can do to help you in your investigation?''

"Can't think of a thing, Senator, but I'm much obliged that you asked.'' Longarm turned his head toward the grandstand and saw a man standing underneath the benches, at the edge of the shadow cast by the grandstand. Even though it wasn't yet noon, the sun was high enough in the sky, and bright enough, so that the line between light and shadow was a sharply defined border. Longarm couldn't see the face of the man standing there except as a dim blur.

But he could sure as hell see the gun in the man's hand as it rose.

"Get down!'' Longarm yelled as he threw himself at Padgett. His left hand caught hold of the politician's arm and hauled him roughly to the side. At the same time, Longarm's right hand was flashing across his body to the butt of the Colt in the cross-draw rig. He went to one knee as he gave Padgett a hard shove that sent the startled senator sprawling on his ass. Longarm heard the crack of a gun, and splinters leaped from the wooden railing above his head as a bullet chewed a hunk from it.

"What . . . what . . .'' sputtered Padgett. Then, as the would-be assassin's gun boomed again, he yelped, "Oh, my God!''

Longarm twisted around and triggered a shot of his own, grimacing as the bullet went high and thudded into the underside of the grandstand. The gunman fired a third and final time, the slug kicking up dust several feet to Longarm's right; then he whirled around and dashed back deeper into the shadows underneath the benches.

Biting back a curse, Longarm reached out with his left hand and pushed Padgett back to the ground as the senator struggled to get up. "Stay down, damn it!'' Longarm barked at him, then surged to his feet. He ran toward the grandstand, the Colt held ready in his hand.

He darted around one of the thick wooden beams that supported the stands and found himself half-blinded by the

48

sudden change from brilliant sunlight to thick shadows. He was confused even more by the narrow shafts of light that slanted down through openings between the benches, not to mention the veritable forest of beams that formed the structural skeleton of the grandstand. If he went running along full-blast before his vision adjusted, he'd be liable to dash his brains out in a collision with one of the support beams.

However, as long as he stood here at the edge of the light, he was a perfect target for the fleeing gunman. A bullet slammed into the beam next to Longarm to punctuate that thought. He crouched and went forward at a slow run, veering from beam to beam.

Unwilling to fire again until he had a good, clear shot, Longarm waited several moments, then triggered his Colt. The bullet whined off to one side of the dimly seen running shape ahead of him. The bushwhacker obviously intended to stay underneath the grandstand until he reached the other end of it.

So far, despite all the powder that had been burned, none of the bullets had hit anything except dirt and wood. That situation didn't change as Longarm's next shot went into the ground behind the darting figure. This was getting downright tiresome, he thought.

The next moment, the ambusher emerged from the shadows into the sunshine. He stumbled a little, and Longarm knew he had to be squinting hard against the glare. Longarm came to a stop, leveled his gun, and squeezed off another shot as the gunman abruptly veered to the side. Longarm's bullet smacked into one of the support beams.

The running figure disappeared, only to be replaced an instant later by a much larger one. The pounding of hoofbeats came to Longarm's ears, echoing underneath the stands. The would-be assassin had had a horse waiting for him.

When Longarm ran out from under the grandstand a moment later, he shielded his eyes with his hand and saw the man riding hard away from the racetrack, already with a good lead. Longarm had come out here this morning in a rented buggy, just as he'd done the day before, and the closest saddle horse was probably Caesar, out on the track itself. There might be other mounts around the paddock area, but it was all the way at the other end of the track. He watched the dwindling figure of the rider, then slid his Colt back into its holster. That gunman wasn't going to be caught today.

"Marshal! Marshal Long!" The agitated voice of Senator Padgett came from behind him.

Longarm turned sharply and saw Padgett hurrying toward him through the alternating bands of light and shadow. "Blast it!" Longarm snapped, ignoring for the moment the fact that the other man was a powerful politician. "I thought I told you to stay out of harm's way!"

Padgett drew to a stop. "I heard more shooting and wanted to make sure you hadn't been hit," he said. "Are you all right, Marshal?"

"Not even a scratch," Longarm said. "How about you, Senator?"

Padgett brushed some of the dust from his coat and trousers. "I don't seem to be hurt, just shocked that such a thing could happen in broad daylight. Was that man trying to kill you?"

"He was aiming at you," Longarm said with certainty. "I saw that much before I knocked you out of the way."

Padgett shook his head, but he wasn't denying what Longarm had said. "Why?" he asked. "Why would anyone want to kill *me*?"

"You're a senator," Longarm reminded him. "Politicians always have plenty of enemies."

"Oh, certainly," Padgett said with a wave of his hand, "men whose bills I've opposed, or who opposed bills of mine, but no one who would . . . would try to murder me! Some cutting comments or a spate of angry rhetoric on the floor of the Senate are as far as they would go."

"You sure about that? I'm not saying one of your fellow senators would come to Albuquerque and take a shot at you himself, but he could hire it done easy enough."

Padgett shook his head again, and this time the motion

was a denial. "Impossible. I don't believe it."

The sound of running footsteps and an anxious voice calling, "Senator! Senator, are you all right?" made Longarm and Padgett both turn around. Cy, the diminutive rider who had been putting Caesar through his paces, was hurrying toward them.

"I'm fine, Cy," Padgett assured the man as Cy came up to them.

"But I heard shots!"

"There was some gunfire," Padgett admitted, "but Marshal Long here frightened off the man who was shooting at us."

Cy gulped. "Lordy! You mean somebody tried to assassinate you, Senator, like that actor fella did to old Abe?"

Padgett grimaced in irritation. "No, I'm certain it was nothing like that," he said. "You go back and tend to Caesar, Cy. You didn't leave him just standing on the track in the sun, did you?"

"Well . . . when I heard the shooting, I figured I'd better see what was going on."

"Damn it, man," Padgett barked, his face flushing angrily. "You can't just leave a fine horse like Caesar standing there when he's hot and sweaty. Get him back to the stable and rub him down, for God's sake!"

Cy nodded jerkily as the harsh words lashed at him. "Yes, sir, Senator. Right away." He turned and practically sprinted back toward the track.

Padgett sighed wearily and turned toward Longarm. "I suppose we'll have to report this incident to the authorities." His angry reprimand of Caesar's rider seemed to be already forgotten.

"Yep, the Albuquerque police will have to know about it," Longarm said. "I reckon I ought to send a wire to Billy Vail and let him know what happened too."

"Is that really necessary?"

Longarm chuckled humorlessly. "You know Billy, Senator. He won't take it kindly if he hears that one of his deputies was mixed up in a shooting with somebody who

51

tried to assassinate a United States senator and said deputy didn't report it his own self.''

Padgett frowned and said, ''Yes, I suppose you're right. I don't much like that word 'assassinate,' though.''

''You're a public figure, Senator. Like it or not, that's what happened here today.''

''Very well. You'll take care of notifying Marshal Vail and the local authorities before you get started on your own mission once again?''

''Sure,'' Longarm said with a nod. ''I'll get a wire off to Denver first thing. Then I'll go see that Captain Bishop. I'll bet he's getting a mite tired of seeing me, since there's always some sort of trouble involved when he does.''

''That's his job,'' Padgett said curtly. ''He's paid to handle trouble.''

''Yes, sir,'' agreed Longarm. ''He sure is.''

And so was a United States deputy marshal.

''Son of a bitch!'' Longarm said as he slapped the open palm of his left hand on the counter in the hotel lobby. His right hand slightly crumpled the yellow telegraph flimsy the clerk had just given him.

The desk clerk swallowed and worked up the nerve to ask, ''Bad news, Marshal?''

''You could say that,'' Longarm replied. He fished his watch out of his vest pocket, flipped it open, and checked the time. It was almost six o'clock. ''When does the southbound train for El Paso pull out?''

''Why, six-thirty, I believe. If it's on schedule, and it usually is.''

''Get my bill ready,'' muttered Longarm. ''I'm leaving.''

He jammed the telegram into his coat pocket and turned toward the stairs. When he reached his third-floor room, he began packing. That didn't take long, since all he had was a few spare clothes, which he stuffed in his war bag, and his Winchester. He had the bag slung over one shoulder and the rifle canted over the other when he came downstairs again. Paying the bill prepared by the clerk took only a moment, and then Longarm strode out of the hotel and headed for the railroad station.

It was only six-fifteen when he got there. The sun was still up, although it rode low enough in the western sky so that its light had taken on a rosy hue. Smoke puffed from the diamond stack of the big locomotive as porters loaded baggage and passengers boarded. As he looked down the line of cars, Longarm saw that ramps had been lowered from several of them to the ground alongside the tracks. Those were the cars where the racehorses, including Senator Padgett's Caesar and the Cassidy sisters' Matador, would be loaded for the trip to El Paso and the next stop on the racing circuit.

Longarm walked through the station lobby and onto the platform, looking for Padgett. He spotted the senator climbing the steps to one of the passenger cars, followed by his assistant, Leon Mercer. Longarm's hands were full, since he was carrying both his war bag and the Winchester, so he settled for calling out, "Senator!"

Padgett stepped up onto the platform at the rear of the car and looked back to see who was hailing him. A look of surprise appeared on his face as he recognized Longarm.

The rangy lawman's long legs carried him across the station platform and up the steps of the railroad car. Padgett said, "What are you doing here, Marshal? I didn't think you were leaving Albuquerque just yet."

"Neither did I," Longarm said curtly. He set his war bag on the car's platform and pulled the telegram from his coat pocket. "But that was before I got this." He held out the yellow flimsy to Padgett.

The politico took the message and read it:

IN LIGHT OF ATTEMPT ON SENATOR PADGETT'S LIFE NEW ORDERS ARE AS FOLLOWS STOP YOU ARE ASSIGNED TO SENATOR AS BODYGUARD UNTIL FURTHER NOTICE STOP PROTECT LIFE AT ALL COSTS STOP VAIL U.S. MARSHAL DENVER.

Padgett looked up at Longarm with a confused frown on his face and asked, "What does this mean?"

Longarm figured Padgett knew what it meant just as well as he did. "It means I'm going with you to El Paso, and then on to Tucson and Carson City and wherever the hell else that racing circuit you've joined up with is going. Unless and until Billy Vail decides otherwise, that is."

"But . . . but I thought you were going after those men who murdered your fellow marshals."

"So did I," Longarm said grimly. "I thought about sending a wire back to Vail and telling him I wasn't going to do it, but I knew if I did, I might as well go ahead and take my badge off for good." He shook his head. "After I thought about it for a while, I figured I wasn't ready to do that."

"Well, this is patently unfair. You want to go after the men who killed your friends, and I don't blame you. Besides, there's no real reason for me to have a bodyguard."

"Someone did try to kill you earlier today, Senator," Leon Mercer pointed out. His tone was rather offended as he went on. "You see, I *told* you you shouldn't have insisted that I stay at the hotel while you went to the racetrack this morning."

Padgett's frown turned to one of irritation. "Damn it, I'm still not convinced that gunman wasn't shooting at you, Marshal Long. I'd think a lawman would be much more likely to have violent enemies than a mere politician."

"Maybe so, but that ain't always the way it is," Longarm said. "Like it or not, Senator, it looks like we're stuck with each other, for a while anyway."

Padgett nodded. "I suppose you're right."

"Well, I for one will be very happy to have the marshal with us," Mercer put in. "I didn't relish the idea of continuing on through the West with bullets whizzing around our heads."

"It wouldn't have come to that—" Padgett began.

He was interrupted by a voice that still seemed soft and sweet as honeysuckle, despite the fact that it had been raised to call out, "Why, Marshal Long, what are you doing here? Did you come to see us off?"

Longarm turned his head and saw Janice and Julie Cassidy standing beside the next car in line. Both young women were wearing simple yet elegant traveling outfits, and they were as lovely today as they had been the day before. Longarm lifted a hand in greeting as Janice hurried down the station platform toward him, followed by Julie.

Janice gathered her skirt and came up the steps at the rear of the car, joining Longarm, Padgett, and Mercer. The relatively small area was getting crowded, but Longarm managed to lift a hand to the brim of his hat as he nodded and said, "Nice to see you again, Miss Janice. Looks like I'm going to be traveling with the senator for a while."

"Oh, how wonderful!" exclaimed Janice. "How did this happen to come about?"

Longarm shot a glance at Padgett and read a warning in the politician's eyes. There had been no witnesses to the attempt on Padgett's life at the racetrack except for Longarm, Cy, and the mysterious gunman himself, of course. Nor would there be any mention of it in the newspaper the next day, so the word wouldn't get out. Longarm had seen to that. He understood what Padgett was trying to tell him: The senator didn't want someone as flighty as Janice Cassidy knowing about what had happened. She would be bound to gossip about it. Longarm agreed with that reasoning.

"My boss has decided I ought to stick close to the senator," Longarm said easily. "Important fellas like him have to have somebody around to look out for them." That was close enough to the truth.

"That sounds perfectly reasonable to me," Julie put in from the station platform. "Come on, Janice, we have to get settled."

Sure enough, as soon as the words were out of Julie's mouth, the conductor came along the station platform, bawling out the traditional " *'Boooarrdd! All aboard!'*"

Janice leaned toward Longarm and brushed her lips across his cheek in a quick kiss. "I'm so glad you're traveling with us, Custis," she murmured throatily. "We're going to have so much fun!"

Longarm refrained from pointing out that he was actually traveling with Senator Padgett, not with Janice and her sister. And he suspected that the second part of her statement was incorrect as well. Given the lusty nature of Janice Cassidy and the hinted-at sensuousness of Julie, this journey around the racing circuit might well have its entertaining moments.

But if he found what he was looking for, it wasn't going to be fun, thought Longarm. No, sir, not much fun at all . . .

Chapter 5

The train was slightly behind schedule as it pulled out on the run from Albuquerque to El Paso. Senator Padgett had a private compartment, befitting his status as an important man, and Longarm intended to share it with him despite the fact that it might get a little crowded with three gents in it. Leon Mercer, of course, was staying close to the senator, although Longarm doubted that the assistant would be much help in case of trouble. Not that Longarm expected another assassination attempt, at least not right away.

Once they had settled down in the compartment, Padgett gave Longarm a cigar, and they both lit up. "Havana," Padgett said, exhaling and wreathing his head in the blue-gray smoke. "Fine, don't you think, Marshal?"

"Well, it's different from those three-for-a-nickel cheroots I usually chew on," allowed Longarm. "Much obliged, Senator."

"Why don't you call me Miles?"

The jovial offer of familiarity had a hollow ring to it, Longarm decided. Like most politicians, Padgett liked to fancy himself a man of the people, just one of the boys, but he actually enjoyed the respect and deference that came with his office. "I reckon Billy Vail would rather I kept things more business-like between us, Senator—but that doesn't mean I don't appreciate the smoke."

Padgett chuckled. "That's all right, Marshal. Whatever you think is best."

Longarm and Padgett were facing each other across the compartment. Mercer sat beside Longarm on the padded bench seat. He had a small valise perched on his lap, and he opened it now to withdraw a sheaf of papers. "I really think you should go over these reports, Senator," he said. "The bills to which they pertain will be coming up for a vote shortly after Congress convenes again in the fall."

Padgett waved the hand holding the Havana cigar, leaving a trail of smoke in the air. "There'll be plenty of time for that later, Leon. Marshal Long, do you really think there's a chance someone will try to kill me again?"

Longarm shook his head and said, "Doesn't matter what I think. It's what Marshal Vail thinks that's important."

"Yes, but you must have an opinion," Padgett pressed.

"Anytime a fella takes a shot at somebody and misses, there's always a chance he'll try again. Of course, there's also a chance that the one time will be the only one he can work up enough gumption for. All I know, Senator, is that you being around all these crowded racetracks will give the fella plenty of opportunity to try again if that's what he wants."

Padgett nodded solemnly. "You're saying that I ought to stop traveling the racing circuit."

Longarm shrugged and said, "It's a thought. You might be safer holed up somewhere."

A bark of contemptuous laughter came from the senator. "Not likely! A man can't be timid in my line of work, just as he can't afford to be timid in yours, Marshal. I have to be out there in front, taking care of my business for all the world to see. Otherwise how can I expect the voters to trust me to take care of the government's business?"

Longarm inclined his head in acknowledgment of Padgett's argument. "So you intend to follow the circuit the whole way?"

"All the way to Denver," confirmed Padgett. He puffed on the cigar. "And I intend for Caesar to win some of the races along the way too."

"It might help if Cy paid more attention to his job," muttered Leon Mercer.

Longarm and Padgett both looked at him in surprise. "Why, Leon," said Padgett, "I don't think I've ever heard you speak ill of anyone. What have you got against Cy?"

"Nothing really, Senator," Mercer replied quickly. "I'm just not sure he's as devoted to winning as you are. I've no doubt he's back in one of the baggage cars with the other jockeys right now, drinking and gambling."

"A man's got a right to associate with his cronies," Padgett said.

Mercer sniffed. "I suppose so. But it seems to me he could devote more time to his job."

"Cy likes to gamble and knock back a drink or two, eh?" said Longarm.

Mercer held up his hands, palms out, and said, "I shouldn't say any more. This . . . this horse-racing business is none of my concern anyway. I've never understood the appeal of watching horses run around and around a track."

Padgett gave another burst of gravelly laughter. "You're just not a competitor, Leon."

"No, sir, I suppose not. Except when it comes to winning elections."

Longarm had the fancy cigar smoked down to a butt. He put it out in the little keg of sand underneath the compartment's window and looked out at the night. There wasn't much to see from here. He stood, stretching his muscles, and said, "Think I'll take a *pasear* up and down a couple of these cars, just to make sure everything's quiet. Lock the door behind me, Senator, and don't open it to anybody except me. I shouldn't be gone long."

Padgett nodded. "All right, Marshal. Don't worry, though. If there is any trouble, I think we can handle it."

With that, he dropped one eyelid in a wink and pulled his coat back a little. Longarm saw the little pistol hanging in a shoulder rig under the senator's left arm. The lawman rubbed his nose to hide the grimace that played quickly across his face. A gun in the hands of a politician was enough to make a fella uneasy. They shot themselves in the foot with their mouths all the time; hard to imagine what damage they might do with an actual firearm.

Longarm nodded and left the compartment. There was nothing else he could do. He was certain he wouldn't be able to talk Padgett into giving up the gun. But it was highly unlikely anything was going to happen, at least tonight.

The senator's private compartment was at one end of a passenger car. Longarm moved down the aisle of the rest of the car, heading toward the rear of the train. The lamps had been turned down, and some of the passengers were already asleep, swaying slightly on the benches from the gentle rocking of the train.

Longarm reached the door at the other end of the car and stepped out onto the platform. Fresh, cool air buffeted his face. This car was far enough back from the engine so that cinders and smoke weren't too bothersome. Longarm inhaled deeply.

The tracks ran just west of the Rio Grande along this stretch. From time to time, the train passed a little cluster of lights that marked one of the farming communities populated mostly by Mexicans. As Longarm stood there enjoying the night air, the tracks began to climb to the pass between the Gallinas Mountains to the west and Gran Quivera to the east. He could see the peaks bulking up darkly in the moonlight. New Mexico wasn't his favorite place in the world, but it did have a certain appeal to it, especially on a night like this with silvery illumination from the moon and stars washing down over the starkly beautiful terrain. It was almost enough to make him forget about the bloody failure of his mission back in Albuquerque.

The door to the next car opened, and Longarm turned his head. A woman's voice said, ''My, it's lovely out here, isn't it?''

Longarm's fingers ticked the brim of his hat. ''Miss Janice,'' he said by way of greeting. ''Or is it Miss Julie?''

To tell the truth, he wasn't sure which of the Cassidy twins had just joined him on the platform, and he didn't see any point in lying about it.

The lovely young woman, whoever she was, laughed softly and closed the door to the other car. She moved over to the platform railing beside Longarm. "It's Julie," she said. "How are you, Marshal Long?"

"Just fine, I reckon. Getting a breath of fresh air."

"That's what I'm doing too. Those train compartments get a little stuffy."

"You and your sister have a private compartment?" One of Longarm's eyebrows lifted in speculation, but it was unlikely Julie would see that in the shadows.

"Janice doesn't particularly like to travel with what she'd call the rabble," Julie said.

"But you don't mind."

She shrugged prettily. "I get along with all sorts of people. In fact, I'd rather spend my time with horse trainers than some of the society types Janice tends to cultivate."

Longarm leaned on the railing and chuckled. "I reckon I'd fall into the category of rabble."

"Oh, but that wouldn't stop Janice from liking you, Marshal." Julie touched his arm lightly. "When it comes to tall, handsome men, Janice is positively egalitarian."

"I grew up hardshell Baptist myself."

She laughed and linked her arm with his. "I just meant she doesn't care what a man does for a living as long as she's attracted to him."

Longarm didn't bother explaining that he had known what she meant. He was a frequent visitor to the Denver Public Library and did quite a bit of reading—especially toward the end of the month when his funds were running low and more expensive pastimes had to wait until he got paid again. He said, "I don't know that your sister's that attracted to me. I reckon she was just being polite."

"I'd say what she did to you in the clubhouse at the racetrack was very polite."

Longarm stiffened in surprise. "Told you about that, did she?"

"We're very close. We always have been. There are no secrets between us, Marshal."

She was very close to *him* at the moment too. Close enough so that he could feel the warmth of her thigh through their clothes as she pressed against him. Close enough so that when she turned a little, the softness of her breast prodded his arm. She reached across her body with her left arm, since her right was still linked with his left, and boldly rubbed the palm of her hand over the front of his trousers.

The memory of what Janice had done to him had already started his manhood to swelling. Julie's brazen caress sent even more blood flowing to it. Her hand slid up and down, making a shiver of pleasure go through him. After a couple of infinitely tantalizing moments of that, her fingers began searching for the buttons of his fly.

"Now, hold on a minute, ma'am," Longarm said.

Deftly, she flipped two of the buttons open, relieving some of the pressure on him. "I intend to hold on," she said huskily as she found two more buttons and unfastened them. That allowed her to reach inside and free his shaft, which sprang boldly erect as the cold night air washed over it. Julie's fingers closed around it, feeling even warmer because of the contrast than they might have otherwise.

What the hell was this, a contest? One of the Cassidy sisters had fiddled with him until he came in her hand, so now the other one had to try? Lordy, maybe Julie intended to *time* him!

He cast a glance at each of the doors leading to the train cars and said, "This is mighty pleasurable, but I ain't sure it's such a good idea, Miss Julie. Folks could walk out here on this platform any time—"

"I don't mind the risk if you don't, Marshal."

Janice and Julie were a lot alike, all right, thought Longarm. The chance of being discovered seemed to increase Julie's excitement, just as it had with Janice. Her breath was coming fast in her throat as she slid her palm maddeningly along the length of his pole. Longarm turned to face her so that at least what she was doing would be shielded from view by their bodies if anybody else stepped out onto the platform.

Then, to his shock, she began sinking in front of him.

She was getting down on her knees, he realized, and he said hurriedly, "Wait a minute, Miss Julie, you're going to get that nice dress of yours dirty!"

"I don't care," she murmured. "I can't let you think that Janice is the only one who's attracted to you."

He felt the hot tickle of her breath against the knob at the end of his shaft, and then the searing heat of her lips as she kissed it. She slid her hand down to the base of his stalk and held on to it tightly as her mouth opened and wetly engulfed the head. Longarm closed his eyes and groaned, his hips twitching as he instinctively delved deeper into the hot cavern of her mouth.

This *was* a competition, no doubt about it. Janice had brought him to a climax with her hand, and now Julie was bound and determined to do that same thing with her lips and tongue. She was well on the way to accomplishing her end too. Longarm's shaft was throbbing and swelling already. Julie's tongue circled him, swiping wetly all around the head of his pole, greedily lapping up the moisture that seeped from him. He shuddered, put one hand on the railing to steady himself, the other hand on her shoulder. He moved it up to her neck, caressing the soft skin under her ear, feeling the slight tickle of strands of hair that had escaped from the arrangement of curls under her hat. One of her hands still held him at the base of his shaft, while the other reached inside his trousers to fondle his sac. Her tight grip had delayed his climax, but he was getting to the point now so that it would take an earthquake to make him hold back—and even *that* might not do the trick.

Her tongue darted against his opening again in a series of butterfly-light strokes, and that was it. Longarm cupped her chin as his seed boiled up the long tunnel of flesh and erupted from it. He felt the muscles of her throat working against the back of his hand as she swallowed, keeping pace with the flood of juices that came from him. Longarm grunted deeply in pleasure, and a moan came from deep within Julie's throat as well. She shuddered as her own climax thundered through her.

Longarm gasped for breath and then blew it out in a deep sigh. His legs were about as shaky as a newborn colt's. Julie licked him clean, her tongue flicking daintily; then, as she buttoned him up again, she said, "My, that was nice, Marshal Long."

"I reckon you . . . ought to call me . . . Custis, Miss Julie."

"Of course. Help me up, Custis."

He took hold of her arms and easily lifted her. She tilted her head back to look into his eyes and smiled at him, then came up on her toes and brushed a kiss across his cheek.

"I hope you won't think I'm completely shameless, Custis. I'm . . . not in the habit of doing things like this."

He cupped her chin again, ran his thumb over the tiny dimple there. "No, ma'am," he said. "I think just as highly of you as I ever did. Never have understood why some folks think that being a mite frisky is something to be ashamed of."

She laughed. "A mite frisky?" she repeated. "Like a fine mare?"

"I suppose you could say that."

"Well, then, I'll take it as a compliment." Abruptly, her mood grew serious. "Why are you really traveling with the senator, Custis? Has there been some sort of trouble?"

The unexpected questions had him off balance for a second, but he recovered his wits quickly. Maybe he had been wrong about Julie's motivation for what she had done. Maybe she figured that while he was still grateful for the French lesson she'd given him, she could get some information from him in return.

But why? Surely she didn't have anything to do with the job that had brought him aboard this train.

Nothing was impossible, Longarm reminded himself. Unlikely sometimes, but not impossible.

Those thoughts flashed through his mind in an instant, so there was only a slight hesitation before he answered,

"Trouble? Not that I know of. I reckon that's why I'm here, just to make sure there ain't any."

"Well, I feel much better knowing that you'll be traveling with us for a while." Her smile was dazzling in the moonlight. "I think I'm really going to enjoy your company."

"The feeling's mutual, Miss Julie," he assured her.

"I have to be getting back to our compartment now. Janice is probably wondering why I've been gone so long." She laughed again. "She'd certainly be surprised if she knew what that breath of fresh air I went out for turned into. Surprised—and disappointed. She'd wish that she could have been here too."

The image that conjured up had Longarm's legs feeling a little shaky again. He gave Julie Cassidy a quick hug, then stood there on the platform and watched her go back into the other car. They were damned lucky no one had interrupted them a few minutes earlier. That would have made for a mighty awkward situation, he thought.

He fished a cheroot from the pocket of his vest and chewed on it as he considered the questions Julie had asked him. He had tried to keep the attempt on Senator Padgett's life as quiet as he could, but it was possible Julie had heard something about it. She wouldn't know the whole story, though, which would explain why she had tried to pump him. But what business was it of hers if somebody took a few potshots at a politician?

Maybe Julie wasn't thinking of Padgett as a politician at all, but rather as a rival racehorse owner. That could explain her interest.

Plenty of questions but no real answers yet . . . Longarm was used to that, maddening though it could be at times. He was just going to have to wait and see what happened.

In the meantime, something that Leon Mercer had said earlier still interested him. Longarm made his way back through the train, heading for the baggage cars. He wanted to see if Mercer had been right about the jockeys.

• • •

"Three beautiful little ladies, boys," Cy was saying as Longarm opened the door to the baggage car. "That means the pot's mine again." He leaned forward to rake in the bills and coins piled in the center of the blanket that had been spread out on the floor of the car.

There was an open space in the center of the car with a narrow aisle leading to it. The rest of the room was taken up by the bags of the passengers. A dozen men were crowded around the blanket, but only half of them were playing cards; the others were just watching. Like Cy, all the other men were short and slender. The biggest of them would only make about two thirds of Longarm.

That made him feel rather large and gawky as he came up to them and nodded pleasantly. "Howdy, fellas," he said. "I heard there was a game back here."

"No room for any outsiders," Cy said curtly. He took a flask from inside his coat, uncorked it, and swallowed a healthy swig of whatever was inside. After wiping the back of his hand across his mouth, he glared up at Longarm and went on. "You big galoots think you can just bull your way in anywhere, don't you?"

"No call to get riled," Longarm told him, making an effort to keep his own tone mild. He could tell that Cy was drunk. "I ain't one to push in where I ain't wanted."

"It's not that we don't want you to play, Marshal," said one of the other jockeys. "There's just not room."

"And if there's not enough room for us short-growed little runts," added Cy, "there's sure as hell no place for a big bastard like you."

Longarm's jaw clenched a little. Surrounded by his fellow jockeys, with a few slugs of Who-Hit-John inside him, Cy was completely different from the way he had been at the racetrack. Longarm could see it plainly on Cy's young face: The jockey was feeling that while he might have to put up with his employer's bullying, he didn't have to take shit from anybody else.

Longarm held up his hands, palm out. "Didn't mean to cause a ruckus. I'll just back on out of here, boys—"

"Boys!" Cy came to his feet as he angrily repeated

Longarm's word. "We're not boys! We're grown men, no matter how little you think we are."

"You're looking for trouble where there ain't none, Cy," Longarm told him. "I already said that if you fellas don't want me here, I'll go on about my business."

Truth to tell, the other jockeys didn't seem that disturbed by Longarm's presence. Cy was the only one so far in his cups, though. He came toward Longarm, the constant motion of the train making him stumble slightly. With an easy, athletic grace that seemed unaffected by the liquor he had drunk, he caught his balance.

"I'm mighty damned tired of you gents who think you're better'n me just because you're taller and weigh more. What do you think of that, Mr. High-and-Mighty Marshal?" Cy was close enough now to prod Longarm in the chest with a finger.

Longarm had been accosted by drunks before, often enough to know that such hombres were usually more annoying than dangerous. A percentage of the time, however, it was unwise to ignore their potential threat, and that percentage was large enough to make Longarm alert. As far as he could tell, Cy wasn't armed; none of the jockeys seemed to be, unless they had hideout guns or knives. Nor was Longarm worried about Cy taking a swing at him. But if all twelve of the jockeys jumped him, that fracas could get a mite tricky.

Luckily, most of the men didn't seem inclined to share Cy's belligerence. In fact, only a couple of them had tensed and leaned forward, as if they intended to jump into the fight if one broke out. Longarm muttered, "The hell with this. I ain't got time for it." He turned, intending to leave the baggage car and make his way back to Senator Padgett's compartment.

Behind him, Cy let out a whoop. The jockey leaped on Longarm's back, wrapping his legs around the lawman's waist. He circled Longarm's neck with his left arm and began pounding his right fist against the side of Longarm's head. "I'll show you!" Cy shouted. "I'm not scared of you just because you're bigger!"

Longarm felt a wave of disgust that the situation had gotten out of hand, along with a pain in his ear where Cy had clouted him. All he had wanted to accomplish by coming back here was to see if Leon Mercer had been right about Cy. It appeared that Mercer had been, in spades.

Reaching behind him, Longarm got hold of Cy's coat. He bent at the waist and heaved at the same time, and Cy flew over his head with a startled yelp. The jockey sailed through the air for a few feet, then crashed into a pile of baggage.

"Get him!" yelled someone from behind Longarm.

He turned quickly and saw one of the other jockeys launching a punch at him. Longarm reached out, put his hand on the fella's head, and shoved him away, holding him at arm's length. The man flailed punches at him, none of them reaching their intended target. "Stop it!" Longarm snapped. "I don't want to fight you!"

Something hit the back of his knees, and his legs folded up. As he twisted around, he saw it was Cy who had tackled him. Cy had recovered from being thrown into the pile of baggage quicker than Longarm had expected him to. A hard punch connected with Longarm's jaw, and a second later a kick caught him in the side.

These jockeys might be small, but they were strong and tough. Just as he had expected, he had his hands full with Cy and the other two. Luckily, the rest of the group was hanging back, watching the scuffle with keen interest but showing no signs of joining in. Longarm drove an elbow into the belly of one man, then backhanded another as he came up onto his knees. Lurching to his feet, Longarm set himself just as Cy drove in again. Longarm met him with a straight right that sent him spinning off his feet. When he checked on the other two, he saw that the fight had gone out of them.

Cy was stunned, but as he blinked up at Longarm, his eyes cleared a little and he said spitefully, "Makes you feel good, don't it, beating up on somebody smaller than you?"

Longarm spat on the floor. "Shit! You want it both ways,

don't you? You act like a jackass and start a fight, then figure I ought to feel guilty for winning just because I'm bigger'n you!" He picked up his hat, pushed the crown back into its normal shape, and clapped it on his head. "I'm done here."

One of the other jockeys chuckled. "Maybe you ought to pick your fights better, Cy. This one doesn't seem to have worked out very well."

"Yeah, yeah," muttered Cy as he sat up and rubbed his aching jaw. Longarm cast a hard look in his direction and turned to walk out of the baggage car.

This time nobody jumped him.

His blood had stopped pumping so hard and his anger had died down a little by the time he reached the platform where he and Julie had had their passionate interlude a while earlier. He was still a little sore at Cy, though, so he paused to take a couple of deep breaths and think about what he had learned. He put both hands on the railing and leaned forward.

The train had come down from the pass and was approaching the high trestle that spanned the canyon of the Rio Grande. The tracks would cross over to the eastern side of the river and stay there until they reached El Paso.

Cy liked to drink, and from the sound of what had been going on when Longarm entered the baggage car, he was quite a gambler too. That didn't have to mean a damned thing; plenty of men liked to play cards and take a little nip now and then. But Cy was evidently filled with a lot of anger and resentment too, and that whole combination could be explosive. Such a man could be ripe for exploitation by someone with deeper, darker motives.

That thought was going through Longarm's mind when he heard a door open behind him. He didn't have time to turn and see who had come onto the platform, nor from which car they had emerged. All he had time for was to hear the sudden rush of air as something came toward his head.

Then what felt like a two-by-four slammed into his skull,

driving him forward against the railing around the platform. He was barely conscious of the hard shove that lifted his feet into the air and sent him flipping over the rail into nothingness.

Chapter 6

He might have passed out for a second or two; Longarm
was never really sure about that. But the feeling of empty
air all around him woke him up in a hurry, and instinct
made him reach out desperately. Both hands closed around
the top of the iron railing around the platform. With a jerk
that nearly wrenched his shoulders from their sockets and
brought a cry of pain from his mouth, his weight hit his
arms. Somehow he managed to hang on.

His hat was gone, and the wind of the train's passage
caught his thick brown hair and whipped it into his eyes.
He could see well enough as he looked up, though, to spot
the shadowy figure of a man on the platform. The hombre
had some sort of club in his upraised hands. Longarm's
thinking was more than a little addled by the unexpected
attack and the impact of the blow to his head, but the part
of his brain responsible for survival was screaming at the
rest of him that the man was about to bring that club down
on his clutching fingers.

Longarm's feet dangled loosely. They would have anyway, since the platform was high enough that his feet
wouldn't touch the ground while he was hanging from the

railing like this. But the echoing clatter of the train's progress told him that they were on the trestle now. There was nothing between him and the Rio Grande far below except a lot of empty space.

The club whipped down, and Longarm jerked the fingers of his right hand away just in time to avoid the blow. But that put all his weight on his left hand, and the muscles and bones in the fingers of that hand cried out in agony. The attacker lifted the club again.

Longarm's right hand closed over his watch chain and jerked the derringer from the pocket of his vest. He grabbed the little gun and lifted it, cocking it as he did so. The derringer cracked spitefully. Over the roar and clatter of the train's wheels, Longarm heard a whine that told him the bullet had missed and had ricocheted off into the night from the iron of the platform.

The crack and flash of the shot was enough to spook his assailant, however. The man turned and plunged back through the door of the car, leaving Longarm hanging alone from the railing. Thankful for small favors, the marshal dropped the derringer and let it dangle at the end of the watch chain. He slapped that hand against the railing again and hung on tightly. Slowly but surely, the muscles in his shoulders bunching and rippling, he began to pull himself up.

He kept his eyes open, in case the attacker showed up again and made another try at knocking him off the train, but no one came onto the platform. Longarm kicked a leg up and managed to get a foothold. He lifted himself higher, gave another heave, and rolled over the railing to sprawl on the thick planks of the platform itself. His pulse was hammering wildly in his head, and his chest rose and fell hugely as he dragged air back into his lungs.

The train was off the trestle by now and was rolling across flat fields alongside the river. After a couple of minutes, Longarm was able to stand up. Recalling another job that had almost been the death of him, he said fervently, "Damn, I hate hanging off trains!"

He climbed rather unsteadily to his feet and looked

around the platform for his hat. It was gone, of course, just as he had expected. No doubt it had sailed off into the Rio Grande. He hoped that the farmer who would no doubt fish it out of the river would enjoy having a snuff-brown, flat-crowned Stetson. It would be a lot worse for wear by then, more than likely.

Longarm ran his fingers through his wind-tangled hair and took a couple more deep breaths. He tucked away the derringer in his vest pocket. He supposed he looked presentable enough. He went into the passenger car and headed for the senator's compartment. Along the way, he looked at the passengers riding on the bench seats. Some were asleep, some read by the dim light of the lamps, others sat and smoked or simply sat. None of them gave him any more attention than an idle glance, and no one made his job any easier by jumping up and confessing to the attempt on his life. That came as no surprise.

Leon Mercer was alone in the compartment when Longarm tried the knob and found it unlocked, despite what he had told Padgett earlier. Mercer had several documents spread out on his lap. He looked up distractedly from his work and said, "Oh, it's you, Marshal."

"Damn right it's me," said Longarm. "Where's the senator?"

"He went to use the, ah, facilities. He said he wouldn't be gone long."

Longarm bit back a curse. "I thought I told him to stay here in the compartment."

Mercer shrugged and said mildly, "I gather that he didn't have much choice in the matter."

"All right, blast it. Which way did he go?"

"I believe it's just at the near end of the next car."

Longarm was still in the doorway of the compartment. He turned and started toward the door leading to the next car. It was only a few steps away, but before he could reach it, the door opened and Senator Padgett came bustling through. He stopped short when he saw Longarm standing there, an angry frown on his face.

"Hello, Marshal," Padgett said.

"Thought I told you to stay in the compartment until I got back." Longarm didn't bother concealing his bad temper. His voice was curt.

Padgett began to frown as well. "I'll thank you not to take that tone with me, sir," he said. "I didn't see any harm in answering the call of nature." He put a hand to his stomach. "My digestion is not what it once was. One of the curses of advancing age, I suppose."

"Maybe so, but I still wish you'd waited."

"Well, no harm done. I'm fine. No one tried to kill me."

"This time," muttered Longarm.

"Granted." Padgett seemed to notice for the first time that Longarm's hat was gone. "You look a bit disheveled, Marshal. Is something wrong?"

Longarm shook his head. "I lost my hat while I was standing out on the platform," he said. "Wind whipped it right off when we were going over that trestle. Last I saw of it, it was headed for the Rio Grande."

Padgett chuckled, but said, "I'm sorry about your loss. I suppose you'll be able to replace the hat in El Paso, though."

"I reckon." Longarm summoned up a rueful grin. "Wonder if Billy Vail would accept an expense voucher for the cost of a new one."

"Knowing Marshal Vail as I do, I wouldn't count on it."

"Me neither. I suppose if all I lose is a hat, I'll have come out all right."

"Indeed. Now, if you'll excuse me . . ."

Longarm had kept the senator jawing out here in the aisle long enough. He opened the door of the compartment again and stood aside. Padgett preceded him into the little room. Longarm stepped inside long enough to say, "These seats only make out into two bunks, so I'll sleep outside on that bench right across from the door. Like I told you before, keep the door locked. Nobody's going to bother you."

"Your confidence makes my mind rest much easier, Marshal."

Longarm couldn't tell if Padgett was being sarcastic or

not. He thought the senator was sincere, but when a fella shaded the truth for a living, like most politicians did, it was hard to be sure about anything.

Once the door was closed and Longarm had heard the lock snap shut, he settled down on the bench he had pointed out to Padgett and Mercer. Since he had it to himself, he was able to partially stretch his legs out and put his head back. He wished he still had his hat so that he could tip it down over his eyes.

That wasn't all he thought about. He replayed the attack in his head. Could Cy have followed him, clouted him over the head with something, then tried to push him off the train? It was possible, Longarm supposed. He hadn't gotten a good enough look at his assailant in the darkness to know for sure how big the fella had been.

But there was someone else whose whereabouts were unaccounted for at the time of the attack, Longarm realized. With the door to the senator's compartment closed, Miles Padgett could have turned the other direction after telling Mercer he was going to visit the facilities in the next car. Padgett could have stepped out there on that rear platform, seen Longarm standing there, and walloped him one. The question was—why would the senator do such a thing?

Considering why Longarm was on this train, he wasn't going to rule out anything.

Sleep claimed him while he was pondering.

The night passed without further incident. Longarm slept fitfully, and when he stood up as the train was pulling into El Paso not long after dawn, his muscles were stiff and sore and he was almost as tired as when he had first dozed off. Still, he had spent worse nights on the trail in the past. A few cups of strong, hot coffee, some bacon and flapjacks, and he'd start feeling human again, he knew.

Senator Padgett and Leon Mercer seemed well rested. Padgett was his usual bluff and hearty self as he and his assistant stepped down to the platform of the El Paso depot followed by Longarm. "What a glorious morning!" Padgett exclaimed.

75

That was true enough, Longarm supposed. The air was clear and cool here in this pocket among the mountains where El Paso was nestled alongside the winding Rio Grande. It would be hot as blazes later in the day, but right now the temperature was downright pleasant. The craggy heights of Mount Franklin loomed to the north of town. Once El Paso had been known as Franklin, and Billy Vail had served with the Ranger company that had been head-quartered here in those days. Longarm had heard his boss spin many a yarn about the adventures he'd had in the Rangers with his old pard, Roaring Bill McDowell. Wild times, Longarm thought.

But these days could be pretty wild too.

"You go on and register us at the hotel, Leon," Padgett told his assistant. "I'm going out to the track with Caesar."

"I'm sure Cy could handle that, Senator," Mercer said.

Padgett shook his head. "I want to see that Caesar's settled in for myself." He smiled. "I know you think I can't manage anything without you, Leon, but I assure you I'll be all right. Marshal Long will be with me, won't you, Marshal?"

"That's right," Longarm said. "After everything that's happened, I don't plan to let you out of my sight very often, Senator."

And Padgett could take *that* any way he wanted to.

"Good morning, gentlemen!"

The lilting greeting made Longarm, Padgett, and Mercer all turn. They saw the Cassidy sisters coming down the platform toward them. Even this early in the morning, after a night spent in a cramped train compartment, they both looked elegant. Janice was dressed in a dark gray traveling gown and matching hat, while Julie wore a denim riding skirt and a short jacket over a white shirt. Longarm wondered idly if the twins ever wore each other's clothes, switching identities, as it were. Given the differences in their personalities, he doubted it—but as he had told himself the night before, anything was possible.

He also wondered if Julie had told her sister about what

76

she and Longarm had done on the platform that had later on nearly turned into a death trap for him.

Padgett tipped his hat as the young women came up to them, as did Mercer. Longarm didn't have a hat to tip, so he settled for nodding and saying, "Mornin', ladies. Did you have a pleasant night?"

"Very pleasant," Julie said, and Longarm saw the faint twinkle in her eyes.

"I slept very well," added Janice.

"I'm on my way out to the racetrack to see that Caesar is suitably ensconced in the paddock," Padgett said. "Would you ladies care to share a buggy with me?"

"That's very kind of you, Senator," Janice replied, "but all I want to see now is a hotel room. Freshening up on a train just isn't satisfactory."

"You look lovely, my dear," Padgett said. "No one would ever know you just disembarked."

"That's very kind of you, Senator, but I'm still going to the hotel."

Julie said, "I'm not. I have to tend to Matador, so I'll be glad to accept your kind offer, Senator."

Padgett beamed. "Excellent! Leon, see about engaging a buggy for us, will you?"

"Of course, Senator," Mercer said. He hurried away, disappearing into the depot lobby.

Longarm cast a glance along the train. To the rear, the horses were being unloaded from the stable cars. There were a dozen animals on the circuit, so the area just to the north of the station where the unloading was taking place was busy. Hooves clattered on ramps as trainers led the animals down from the cars. The jockeys were bustling around as well. Longarm spotted Cy, who had a bruise on his jaw where Longarm's fist had landed. Longarm wondered if Cy was going to say anything to Senator Padgett about the fracas in the baggage car the night before. He doubted it; Cy was already in the senator's doghouse for losing the race in Albuquerque, and admitting that he'd been brawling with a federal lawman would just make things worse for him. If Cy didn't say anything about it, Longarm didn't intend to either.

Padgett turned to Longarm and asked, "Will you be coming with us, Marshal?"

Before he could answer, Janice took his arm. "Or would you rather help me get settled in at the hotel, Custis?"

Longarm had to grin as he gently disengaged his arm from her grasp. "An offer like that's mighty hard to refuse, ma'am . . . but I reckon I'd better stick with the senator for now."

Janice sighed dramatically and said, "You men! Always worried about something that's not even going to happen! Why, no one would bother the senator. He's too important for that."

"Just a matter of policy, Miss Janice. Fella like the senator's got to have somebody looking after him."

"Damn it, you don't have to make it sound like you're my nursemaid, Marshal," snapped Padgett.

"No offense, Senator. Didn't mean it like that."

Padgett was a little mollified. He nodded and said, "Here comes Leon. That must mean he's found a buggy and a driver for us."

Sure enough, Mercer had engaged an open buggy and a gent named Juan to handle the team. The party went through the depot lobby, and Padgett, Julie, and Longarm climbed into the buggy. Nearby, the bags belonging to Padgett and Mercer, along with Longarm's war bag and Winchester, were being loaded into a flatbed wagon by a couple of porters. Mercer would take the baggage to the hotel and register, as Padgett had ordered. He turned to Janice, tipped his hat again, and asked, "Would you like to have me take care of your bags as well, Miss Cassidy?"

"That would be very kind of you, Mr. Mercer," replied Janice as she favored him with a dazzling smile. "In fact, I'll even ride to the hotel with you on the wagon."

Mercer's eyes widened in surprise, and he stammered, "Th-that's not necessary, ma'am. I'm s-sure you'd be more comfortable in a carriage."

"Nonsense." Janice linked her arm with his. "I'll be

glad to join you. I've always thought you were such a dear man.''

Mercer blushed a bright pink to the roots of what sparse hair he had left. Longarm had to swallow a laugh at the stricken look on the man's face. Mercer obviously wasn't accustomed to much female attention, especially from a female as lovely as Janice Cassidy.

As Janice led Mercer away, Padgett leaned over toward Longarm and asked in a half-whisper, "Do you think Leon will be safe?"

"I don't reckon Miss Janice will get too frisky in broad daylight, in the middle of downtown El Paso."

But at the same time, given the lady's history, he couldn't completely count on that. . . .

Within a quarter of an hour, the racehorses had all been saddled and their jockeys were aboard for the ride out to the track. The horses were trailed by buggies carrying their owners, trainers, and assorted hangers-on. Longarm supposed he would fall into that last category. They made quite a procession as they followed the road that ran roughly parallel to the border river. On the other side of the river were the shanties of Juarez town, and behind them rose hills and mountains that were in Mexico. The caravan of racehorses and buggies headed northwest, toward the corner where Texas, New Mexico, and Mexico all butted up against each other. The big racetrack was located on the outskirts of El Paso, still in Texas, just across the borders from its neighbors.

Longarm rode in the buggy's rear seat, while Senator Padgett shared the front seat with Julie Cassidy. If Longarm hadn't been here to work, he would have preferred being up there with Julie. As it was, he caught several glances she threw over her shoulder at him, and from the smoldering looks she gave him, he knew they were both thinking about the same thing.

Not that cavorting with the beautiful Miss Cassidy was the only thing on his mind. He hadn't forgotten about the attempt on his life the night before. The ache in his hands, arms, and shoulders wouldn't let him forget.

The only thing he could be sure of was that whoever had tried to kill him wasn't the same fella who had taken those shots at Senator Padgett back in Albuquerque. His primary suspect was Cy, or perhaps one of the other jockeys who had come out on the short end—so to speak—of that fight. But Padgett had been unaccounted for at the same time, and that fact gnawed at Longarm's brain. Padgett had understood that he was supposed to remain in the compartment. He must have had a compelling reason to ignore what Longarm had told him. Needing to pay a visit to the facilities could be pretty compelling, all right.

But so was murder.

Longarm was still puzzling over it when the racetrack came into view. The track itself was the same size as the one in Albuquerque, but the grandstands were larger and more impressive. Longarm estimated that they might hold twice as many people as the stands at the other track. That could make it more difficult for him to keep up with everybody he wanted to watch, but he would just have to make the best of it. At this point, there was nobody he trusted enough to bring in on the job with him.

For the next hour, Longarm tagged along behind Padgett as the senator oversaw Caesar going through a brief exercise run, then being settled in one of the stalls in the paddock. Cy avoided meeting Longarm's eyes anytime the jockey was around him. By the time Padgett was satisfied that everything had been taken care of properly, Longarm's stomach was growling. He was still waiting for that coffee, bacon, and flapjacks. He hoped the hotel dining room would still be serving breakfast by the time they got there.

"Come along, Cy," Padgett said to the jockey, motioning for him to follow along to the buggy. "You can ride with Marshal Long and me back to town."

Cy stiffened and looked at Longarm, who lifted his shoulders in a little shrug. Padgett didn't seem to have noticed the bruise on Cy's jaw; if he had seen it, he had chosen not to say anything about it. "Sure," Cy responded after a second's hesitation. "Thanks, Senator."

Longarm climbed into the front seat beside Padgett this time, and Cy settled himself in the back. The serape- and sombrero-clad driver picked up the reins and got the buggy's two-horse team moving. The trip back to downtown El Paso did not take as long as the one out to the racetrack.

"What about Miss Cassidy?" asked Longarm as they rolled toward the center of the sprawling border settlement. "Won't she need a ride back to town too?"

"Julie won't have any trouble getting to the hotel. But she'll be at the track most of the day. She really hates to leave that horse. I think she cares more about Matador than anyone else."

Longarm raised an eyebrow. "What about her sister?"

"All Janice cares about is winning. . . . Oh, I see what you mean. You're asking if Julie cares more about her sister than she does about Matador. Well, of course. The Cassidy sisters are devoted to each other. They're close, very close." Padgett chuckled, and a hint of a leer appeared on his face as he said conspiratorially, "In fact, some of the stories I've heard about those two—"

"Are probably just cheap gossip," Longarm finished for him before Padgett could go on.

Padgett glanced at him, clearly puzzled by Longarm's reaction and unsure whether or not he should be offended by the lawman's tone. Evidently he decided it wasn't worth it, because he merely grunted and leaned back against the buggy seat.

Longarm was a mite puzzled by the sharp words that had come from his mouth too. Julie and Janice didn't need him to defend them. They were both outspoken enough to take up for themselves if the need arose. Besides, given the lusty nature of both young women, there might well be some truth to what Padgett had implied.

But it had just sounded so damned sordid coming from the senator, Longarm decided. That was why he'd reacted as he had.

The incident seemed to be forgotten by the time the buggy reached the Camino Real Hotel a few minutes later. The place had the best accommodations in town, which came as no surprise to Longarm. Someone like Miles Padgett would stay in only the best hotels. The Cassidy sisters and the other horse owners were staying there as well. Longarm hoped there would be room for him too. If not, he would simply have to make room.

But it was a good thing that Uncle Sam would ultimately wind up paying for this, Longarm thought with a grin as he followed Padgett into the fancy lobby. He could never afford to stay in a place like this on a deputy marshal's wages.

Leon Mercer was waiting for them inside, and explained that he and the senator had adjoining rooms on the second floor. "I got you the room across the hall, Marshal," he said to Longarm. "That was the best I could do."

"Not quite," said Longarm. "You'll take the room across the hall, and I'll bunk in the one next to the senator."

"Impossible. I have to be on hand to assist Senator Padgett—"

"It's all right, Leon," Padgett told him. "You'll be right across the hall if I need you."

Mercer sniffed. "Well, I don't like it, but I suppose the arrangement will have to do."

"How was your ride with Miss Janice?" asked Longarm, unable to resist needling the stuffy assistant a bit.

Another flush spread across Mercer's features. "Miss Cassidy is quite . . . quite a lovely young lady."

"She sure is," agreed Longarm. He was willing to bet that Janice had flirted with Mercer every foot of the way and had enjoyed every minute of it.

Longarm's war bag and repeater had already been taken up to the room. He checked on them, moved the bag and rifle across the hall to the room adjoining Senator Padgett's, then carried Mercer's bags over to the other room. Mercer watched with poorly concealed resentment. He had to feel as if Longarm was poaching on his territory, namely the senator. Mercer would just have to get over it, though. This assignment of Longarm's wouldn't last forever, only until he found out what he needed to know.

The hotel dining room was indeed still serving breakfast.

Longarm sat down with Padgett and Mercer and proceeded to put himself on the outside of everything he had thought about earlier, plus a small army of fried potatoes. Just as he had expected, he felt like a new man when the meal was finished—a well-stuffed, drowsy man.

But there was work to do, and a last cup of coffee—spiked with a healthy dollop of Maryland rye from a bottle that the waiter brought in from the bar next to the dining room—perked up Longarm enough so that he thought he could make it through the day.

He started by asking Senator Padgett what his plans were. "I'm going to take it easy today," Padgett replied as he fired up one of those Havana cigars. He didn't offer one to Longarm this time. "Tomorrow I'm supposed to make a courtesy call on the mayor of El Paso, but today I intend to rest."

That sounded good to Longarm too, but he didn't have time for it. "Go to it," he told Padgett. "Just lock your door and don't go wandering around."

"What will you be doing, Marshal?"

"Thought I'd look up an old friend or two whilst we're here. Don't worry, Senator. I can almost guarantee that nobody will take a shot at you again."

"Almost guarantee? What do you mean by that?"

"I think that fella from Albuquerque is long gone. He didn't expect anybody to shoot back at him. I could tell he was mighty spooked when I returned his fire. Could be he ain't even stopped running yet."

Padgett laughed. "I sincerely hope you're right, Marshal. Very well, I'll be in my room if you need me. I assume Mercer is allowed to work with me?"

"Sure," Longarm said with a casual wave of his hand. "I don't think it's very likely *he's* the one out to kill you."

The senator looked pained for a second, as if he wished Longarm hadn't reminded him that he was targeted for death. But then the familiar cocky grin reappeared on his face, and he headed upstairs with Leon Mercer trailing him. The assistant was already talking about those legislative reports the two of them needed to go over.

Longarm needed some information too, but not the kind he could get from a report prepared by some fella like Mercer who practically had to be dragged away across the Potomac. What Longarm needed was to find out where the high-stakes card games were held in this town.

But as he turned toward the front entrance of the hotel, he saw Cy slipping out the back. There was definitely something furtive about the jockey's movements.

A grin spread across Longarm's face. Maybe he wouldn't have to go in search of the information he wanted.

Maybe Cy would lead him right to it.

Chapter 7

Longarm gave Cy time to get a little lead on him, then walked quickly through the hotel bar to the rear entrance. He stepped out onto a side street and looked in both directions. It was a little difficult to pick out Cy's figure among the pedestrians along the busy street, since for the most part the Mexican inhabitants of El Paso were both shorter and more slender than the whites. Longarm spotted the checked shirt Cy was wearing, though, about a block and a half away. He walked after the jockey, not hurrying now. He didn't want to get too close.

Cy turned right at the corner, which took him straight toward the Rio Grande. Maybe he was going over to Juarez, Longarm thought. That brought a frown to his face. He had been to Juarez several times in the past, and he'd been shot at there more than once. Not only that, but he'd never gotten along very well with the Mexican authorities either, probably because of the times when circumstances had led him to give a hand to various groups rebelling against the dictatorship of Porfirio Diaz. The common folks on the other side of the border liked Longarm and called him Brazo Largo; more than one lawman over there would have been happy to see him in front of a firing squad.

As it turned out, Cy wasn't bound for Mexico after all. He stopped at a three-story frame building that housed a saloon and brothel. Longarm recognized the structure. He'd been there before, when it had been called the Antelope Saloon. Obviously it had changed hands since then, because now it was the Crystal Star.

As Longarm headed toward the big saloon, he cast a glance at a shop he passed. Displayed in the window were several Stetsons, including one like the hat he'd lost on the train. But he couldn't stop long enough to buy a replacement now. He had to make sure Cy wasn't just ducking through the Crystal Star in order to throw anybody who was following him off the trail.

That wasn't the case at all, Longarm saw a few moments later as he paused just outside the establishment's batwing doors. Cy was at the bar, lifting a mug of beer to his mouth.

A good-sized saloon in a border town never really closed. Drinkers would be at the bar twenty-four hours a day, and the roulette wheels, the poker tables, and the faro layouts would never shut down. There would be a nearly steady stream of traffic up and down the stairs leading to the second and third floors where the bar girls plied their other occupation. But there were slack times, and this mid-morning hour was one of them. There were less than a dozen men at the bar, and only half the tables were occupied. That would make Longarm more conspicuous if he went inside, he realized. It might be better for him to keep an eye on Cy from out here on the boardwalk in front of the saloon.

Cy downed the mug of beer hurriedly and asked for another. A drink juggler in a wrinkled vest, limp tie, and soiled shirt drew the beer, cut the foamy head off with a paddle, and shoved the mug across the bar to Cy. The jockey seemed content to nurse this one along, and since the place was not busy at the moment, the bartender was content to let him do just that.

After a few minutes, though, Cy motioned for the bartender to come closer, and he leaned across the bar to speak quietly to the man. It was difficult for Longarm to judge expressions in the dim light, but he thought the bartender looked skeptical at first. Then whatever Cy was saying convinced the man, because he nodded and jerked a thumb toward a door at the end of the bar.

Hallelujah, thought Longarm. It was about time he got a break in this case.

Carrying the mug of beer, Cy went to the door, knocked on it, then spoke to whoever called out to him from the other side. The door swung open, just wide enough for Cy to slip through, then closed behind him.

Mighty interesting, Longarm told himself. The rangy lawman pushed through the batwings and ambled toward the bar.

The bartender saw him without really seeing him. Longarm was just another nameless, faceless drinker to the man. "What'll it be?" he asked.

"Beer," said Longarm. "Is it cold?"

"Coldest in El Paso," the bartender replied listlessly, obviously not believing the testimonial and not caring if Longarm believed it either. He drew the beer, cut off the head, and pushed the mug across the bar. "Six bits."

Longarm dropped a silver dollar on the bar and watched it disappear like magic. No change was forthcoming, nor had he expected any. Longarm lifted the mug to his lips and took a swallow. The beer was middling cool and not too bitter.

Not wanting to hurry things along too much, Longarm let the bartender drift away to wait on other customers while he sipped the beer. Eventually, the bartender worked his way back along the hardwood, and as Longarm drained the mug, the man asked, "Another?"

"Believe I will. Thanks." Longarm waited until the mug had been refilled and paid for, then said idly, "Is there anywhere around here a man can sit in on a game of cards?"

The bartender frowned at him for a second, then laughed. "Hell, mister, look around the room. There's a couple of games going on right behind you."

Longarm shook his head without looking around. "I ain't talking about some cowpokes playing penny-ante. I'm looking for a real game."

"Kind of early in the day for that, isn't it?"

"The gents I'm talking about don't rightly care if it's day or night, so long as the cards are being shuffled and dealt." Longarm took a twenty-dollar gold piece from his pocket and casually tapped it against the edge of the bar. "You know the sort of fellas I mean."

The bartender grunted. "Yeah, maybe," he allowed. "Anybody in particular tell you to come here?"

Longarm didn't want to risk coming up with a phony name. The bartender would likely see right through that. He said, "Nope. I just heard talk around town that the Crystal Star usually has a good game going on."

"Could be." The man's eyes licked over the gold piece in Longarm's hand like the tongue of a thirsty man in the desert when he spots a water hole.

Longarm slid the coin across the bar. "I'd admire to know for sure."

The drink juggler's fingers covered the gold piece as he inclined his head toward the door at the end of the bar. "Down there. Knock and tell 'em Casey said it was all right."

"Much obliged," Longarm said with a smile. Carrying his mug of beer, as Cy had before him, he sidled along the bar toward the door.

A man's voice answered his knock. "Yeah?"

Longarm put his head close to the door and said, "Casey sent me back here."

The panel opened, and the guard inside said, "Big 'un, ain't you?"

"Back home they called me a runt," Longarm replied, grinning, as he stepped through the door. The guard shut it behind him.

This man was definitely not a runt. He stood a couple of inches taller than Longarm, and his shoulders were even broader than the lawman's. His bullet-shaped head was covered with very close-cropped gray hair. The thick ridge above his bushy eyebrows and the misshapen ears told Longarm the guard had spent a considerable amount of time in a prizefight ring. The dullness that glazed the eyes of many such men was missing in this fella, however. His gaze was sharp and surprisingly intelligent as he ran it over Longarm.

After a second, he pointed to another door at the end of a short hall. "Go through there. It'll cost you a hundred to buy in."

"No problem," Longarm assured him. He had a hundred dollars in his pockets—barely. It was expense money, intended to last him the whole assignment. Billy Vail would pitch a fit if Longarm lost the whole wad and had to wire him for more. But Longarm didn't plan on that happening.

He went to the other door, opened it, and stepped into a smoky, windowless room lit by a single lamp hanging over the center of a baize-covered table. It could have been high noon or black midnight outside, and in here no one would ever know the difference. Five men sat around the table. None of them looked up from the cards in their hands, even when Longarm eased the door shut behind him with a click. Cy sat to Longarm's left. There was an empty chair directly in front of Longarm; then Cy was ensconced in the first chair going around the table clockwise. To Cy's left was a youngster dressed in cowhand garb who was sweating heavily. Across the table from the empty chair was a man in the frock coat and silk hat of a professional gambler. To his left sat two men in dusty black suits who might have looked like preachers had they not been staring at the cards in their hands and clenching cigars between their teeth.

"I call," said the young cowpoke. He tossed coins into the pot and laid down his cards. "Three tens."

The gambler laughed and tossed in his hand. "Beats me, kid."

The men in black shook their heads and threw in their cards. That left Cy, who laughed and said, "Sorry. Three ladies." He laid down the queens.

The cowboy grimaced and shook his head. The pot

wasn't too sizable, but his eyes still followed it with long-ing and regret as Cy raked it in.

Longarm said, "Looks like Lady Luck's riding with you, friend. Mind if I buy into the game?"

Cy glanced up at him, and it took all of his poker-playing skill to keep his face impassive, Longarm figured. Recognition and fear flickered for an instant in Cy's eyes; then he shrugged and said, "I'll be glad to take your money too, mister."

Clearly, he didn't want Longarm revealing that they knew each other. From the looks of the piles of coins and bills in front of each man, Cy had been winning steadily ever since he had joined the game. Since he was already winning, why would he care if the other players knew that he and Longarm were acquainted? The two of them couldn't be accused of working together to cheat when Longarm hadn't even been there.

Maybe there was some connection between Cy and one of the other men that he didn't want Longarm to know about. Maybe Cy was working for one of those black-suited gents and this was his way of getting his payoff. Come to think of it, there *was* something familiar about both of those soberly dressed gentlemen. Longarm gave them a friendly nod as he sat down in the empty chair. "Howdy, boys," he said. He didn't offer his name.

He didn't have to, because one of the men suddenly gasped, "Shit! It's Longarm!" and went for his gun.

Longarm knew what it meant when the man's hand darted underneath his coat. The other man in black was following suit. Longarm came up out of the chair, moving so fast that the seat overturned behind him. His fingers wrapped around the butt of the .44 and slid it smoothly from the cross-draw rig. The room abruptly reverberated with the deafening thunder of gunshots.

Longarm's first round went into the chest of the man who had recognized him, knocking him backward over the chair from which he had risen in a half-crouch. He died without getting a shot off. The second man fired, but he rushed his aim and the slug whipped harmlessly past Longarm's ear to thud into the wall behind the lawman. Longarm aimed for the fella's right shoulder, hoping to wing him and take him prisoner so that he could find out what this was all about. But the man darted to the side just as Longarm squeezed the trigger, and the bullet caught him at the base of the throat. He staggered back but stayed on his feet somehow as blood fountained from the wound. The gun in his hand started to come up again for another shot. His hand shook wildly—but in these close quarters, even a wild shot could be deadly.

With a curse, Longarm fired again. The bullet bored into the man's forehead and drove him backward against the wall. He dropped the gun and pitched forward onto his face, dead.

Cy, the young cowboy, and the gambler had all gone diving for cover when the guns came out. The jockey was the first one to lift himself from behind the table, and from the corner of his eye Longarm saw that Cy had a little pistol clutched in his hand. Longarm didn't wait to find out what Cy intended to do with the gun. He took a half-step that brought him within arm's reach of the jockey and swatted him with a sweeping backhand. The blow knocked Cy completely off his feet and flung him against the other wall. As he bounced off, Longarm plucked the little pistol from his fingers. Cy would have fallen had he not caught hold of the back of a chair to prop himself up.

"That's it!" snapped Longarm. "Everybody just hold it! The shooting's over!"

"Whatever you say, mister," came the voice of the cowboy. He peeked over the edge of the card-littered table.

"That goes double for me, sir," added the gambler. He didn't even show his head.

Longarm stepped back against the door into the room. As long as he couldn't see the cowboy and the gambler, he didn't fully trust them not to have guns in their hands. "Show yourselves, both of you!" he barked.

They stood up slowly, empty hands held where he could see them. Cy was still holding on to the back of the chair, head down as he shook it groggily.

With no warning, the door slammed against Longarm's back, knocking him toward the table. He sprawled half onto it, scattering cards and coins and greenbacks. As he tried to roll over and get back to his feet, he cursed himself for forgetting about the guard right outside in the hall. The big man had heard the shooting, of course, and had come busting in to see what was going on. Longarm rolled onto his back and saw the bruiser leaning toward him, a snarl on his face, hamlike hands outstretched toward Longarm's neck. Obviously the guard intended to bounce him around a little, then sort everything out later.

And Cy, who had recovered his wits, intended to take advantage of the opportunity to get out of there. He straightened and darted toward the now-open door.

Longarm brought his leg up and dug the toe of his boot into the guard's groin. He had a near-perfect angle for such a blow. The kick landed solidly, and the guard howled in pain, forgetting all about reaching for Longarm's throat. His hands dropped to his crotch instead.

However, the momentum of his charge still carried him forward, and he sprawled heavily on top of the table—and on top of Longarm as well. The legs of the table gave out, snapping and splintering under the weight. The whole shebang crashed to the floor.

Longarm had the breath knocked out of him, and he was pinned down by the guard. Cursing raggedly as he gasped for air, Longarm grabbed the man's shoulders and rolled him to the side, grunting with the effort required to do so. He stumbled to his feet and heard the door at the other end of the hall slamming open. That would be Cy leaving, Longarm knew.

Somehow Longarm had managed to hang on to his gun, so he didn't have to look for it amid the wreckage of the table. He ran out of the room, and a couple of long strides took him through the hall to the other door. He plunged through it.

The shooting in the back room must have sounded like a war breaking out. It had sure as hell cleared the main room of the saloon. Only the bartender remained, and he was crouched behind the bar. The batwings were swinging back and forth violently. Longarm figured that Cy had just batted them aside on his way out.

"Did you see which way that little fella turned when he ran out?" Longarm flung at the bartender.

The man raised up from behind the bar just enough to wave an arm to the left. "That way! Toward the river!"

Longarm bit back another curse. If Cy reached Juarez, he could easily lose himself in that rat's nest of streets over there.

Longarm slapped through the batwings and turned left. He heard several startled shouts ahead of him and saw that Cy had knocked a couple of people down in his headlong flight. Longarm gave chase and said, "Sorry, ma'am," as he passed an angry *mamacita* who had been knocked off her feet by the fleeing jockey. The woman shook a pudgy fist at Longarm's back and threw a string of fluent Tex-Mex curses at him.

Cy had a lead, and he was fast, no doubt about it. But he was accustomed to running his races on horseback, not on foot. Not only that, but each of Longarm's strides made two of Cy's, and the marshal's low-heeled boots didn't slow him down any. Steadily, he closed the gap between them. It helped that Cy was clearing a path for Longarm too.

Cy threw several frightened glances over his shoulder and saw Longarm closing in on him. They were now less than a block from the long wooden bridge over the Rio Grande. Cy put on an extra burst of speed, but it wasn't enough. Longarm reached out, snagged his collar, and hauled back. Cy stumbled, slowing down abruptly, and Longarm practically trampled him. They wound up with Cy sprawled in the dust of the street and Longarm straddling him. Longarm reached down, got hold of Cy's shirt with both hands, and lifted him easily. After shaking him like a terrier for a second, Longarm shoved him back toward the Crystal Star. "Come on," growled Longarm. "Let's go straighten this mess out."

The local law was waiting inside the saloon by the time

Longarm and Cy got there. As Longarm prodded the jockey inside, the bartender pointed at him and said excitedly, "There he is! That's him!"

The two men who had been talking to the bartender swung around to face Longarm. They wore town suits, and each of them held a shotgun. They looked as if they knew how to use the greeners. Each man had a star pinned to the lapel of his coat.

Longarm had holstered his Colt and was glad of that fact; he didn't want any trigger-happy local badge blazing away at him with a scattergun. Before either of the men could say anything, he told them, "Take it easy, boys, we're on the same side. I'm a deputy United States marshal. Name's Custis Long, and I'll be glad to let you see my bona fides if you won't shoot me when I go to reaching for 'em."

"Federal man, eh?" grunted one of the El Paso star-packers. "Guess we'd better see that identification, Long."

Longarm took the wallet containing his badge and papers from inside his coat and handed it to the man. After looking inside the wallet, the man handed it back to Longarm and said, "I reckon you're who you say you are. What the hell was this all about, Marshal Long? And who's this?" He gestured at Cy.

"This fella's my prisoner, at least for the time being," Longarm said.

"I didn't do anything," whined Cy. "Marshal Long's just out to get me!"

"Shut up," said the local lawman. "I'm waiting, Marshal."

"Here's how it was," Longarm began. "I was keeping an eye on this fella here, and when he bought into a high-stakes poker game in the back room yonder, I did too. But a couple of the other players knew me from somewhere, and they had to be nursing a grudge against me for some reason. They hauled out their hoglegs and started shooting at me." Longarm shook his head regretfully. "I tried to take the second fella alive, but I wound up having to kill him too."

"You didn't recognize either of them?"

"Not right offhand. But they sure knew me."

"Let's take a look. My name's Tom Bolt, by the way. I'm the city marshal here. This is my deputy, Dave Singletary."

"Pleased to meet you both." Longarm kept a hand fastened firmly on Cy's collar as the little group started toward the back room. "Come on."

"I tell you, I didn't do anything—"

A jerk from Longarm silenced the jockey for the moment.

Longarm was debating how much to tell Bolt and Singletary about the job that had brought him here. He didn't want to get Senator Padgett mixed up with the local law if it could be avoided. Longarm preferred to play a lone hand until he discovered what he was looking for. Then he could call in reinforcements if it was necessary. He had already admitted that he was keeping tabs on Cy, but he wouldn't go into any details about why. If the local lawmen pressed him, he could say truthfully that it was a federal matter.

The door to the hall leading to the back room was open. Before Longarm and the others reached it, the burly guard came out, walking gingerly and bending over a little. When he saw Longarm, he straightened, his aching family jewels evidently forgotten in the rage that swept through him. "You!" he growled. "I'll—"

Marshal Bolt lifted his shotgun as the guard started forward, fists clenched. "You won't do a damned thing except stand there and behave yourself, Oscar," Bolt said. "That fella you want to pound on is a federal lawman."

"I don't care if he's Queen Victoria's illegitimate son," Oscar said, holding himself back with a visible effort. "The son of a bitch kicked me in the balls!"

Longarm said, "I might not have done that, old son, if you hadn't acted like you wanted to tear my arms off and whale me over the head with 'em."

"I heard shootin' back there—"

"And you didn't stop to find out what had happened," Longarm broke in. "You just came busting in there ready to beat the hell out of anybody you could lay your hands on.''

Oscar glowered at him for a moment, then shrugged. ''Well . . . maybe. It's my job to keep things peaceful back there, and the quickest way to stop a ruckus is to bang a few heads together.''

''There won't be any more of that,'' Bolt said. ''Now, let's take a look at those dead men.''

They all filed into the back room, Cy still dragging his feet so that Longarm had to shove him along. There was no sign of the cowboy or the gambler, which came as no surprise to Longarm. They must have cleared out right after he'd gone in pursuit of Cy, well before the arrival of the local badges. Neither of them would have wanted to get mixed up in the aftermath of this corpse-and-cartridge session, which after all had had very little to do with them.

The bodies of the two black-suited men were still sprawled on the floor, the one Longarm had shot in the throat lying in a pool of drying blood. The other man's shirt and vest were stained crimson, but that was all. Using the toe of his boot, Bolt rolled over the corpse that was lying on its face. He studied the features of both men for a moment, then said, ''I don't think I know 'em. How about you, Dave?''

''Might have seen 'em around town, Marshal, but I don't know their names or why they'd try to gun down Uncle Sam here,'' replied Singletary.

''Guess I'd better check their pockets for identification,'' said Bolt with a sigh. That was going to be a bloody job.

''No need,'' said Longarm. He had been staring at the faces of the dead men, and a couple of names had popped into his head. He dredged up the rest of the memories that went with the names. ''That one's Ned Collier.'' He pointed at the man who had first recognized him. ''And the other one's Ash Benson. They robbed a trunk full of negotiable government securities off a stagecoach up in Colorado a couple of years ago. The securities were being carried on the stage so that anybody who was after 'em would be thrown off the trail, seeing as how such things

96

usually go by train with an official courier. Nobody counted on the stage being held up by a couple of second-rate road agents like Ned and Ash here. That was the start of a string of good luck for those boys. I chased 'em for six months and never got close enough to lay hands on 'em.'' Longarm shook his head. ''Their luck ran out, though. Still, they'd cleaned themselves up a heap, and I might not have recognized them if they hadn't gone to shooting at me.''

''You're sure about this?'' asked Bolt.

''Damn sure. You can wire Chief Marshal Billy Vail in Denver, and he'll confirm everything I've told you. The case against these two was still open.''

Singletary laughed and said, ''Looks to me like you slammed it shut, Marshal.''

''Yeah, I reckon. Am I free to go?''

Bolt nodded. ''I suppose so. Will you be in town for a while?''

''Three days,'' Longarm said. ''I'm staying at the Camino Real.''

The city marshal quirked an eyebrow at that, but he didn't question why a fellow lawman—surely underpaid, as all lawmen were—was staying at the town's fanciest hotel.

''We'll be in touch if we need to talk to you again.''

Longarm nodded and tugged on Cy's collar. ''Come on, old son. You and me got to have a talk.''

Chapter 8

"You can let go of me now," Cy complained when they reached the street. "I'm not going to run off again. I know I can't get away from a long-legged galoot like you."

"You know, I could've just shot you instead of chasing you down," Longarm pointed out. "When you ran out of that saloon, you became a federal fugitive."

"I haven't broken any laws, damn it! Why are you persecuting me, Long?" He let out a groan. "As soon as I saw you sit down at the table, I knew you'd come there to make life miserable for me. I was hoping you'd just pretend that you didn't know me!"

"Take it easy," Longarm said coldly. "I ain't going to argue with you here on the street." He released Cy's collar. "I'd rather just have the answers to some questions."

The jockey sighed. "Go ahead and ask whatever you want. I don't want you to start beating on me again."

Longarm's jaw clenched as he reined in his temper. "I don't recall ever hitting you without a damned good reason, mister. Were you planning to shoot me when you pulled the gun back there in the Crystal Star?"

Cy shook his head and said, "Of course not. I just

wanted to be able to protect myself in case *you* tried to shoot *me*. I know you've got it in for me.''

''Maybe with damned good reason. Somebody clouted me on the head last night and tried to push me off that train as it was crossing the Rio. Happened right after that fracas I had with you and your pards in the baggage car.''

Cy stopped short and stared at Longarm, appearing thunderstruck. ''You think *I* tried to kill you last night?''

''The thought crossed my mind,'' Longarm replied dryly as he motioned Cy into the doorway of an empty store so that they would be out of the way of the pedestrians passing along the boardwalk. ''You strike me as the sort of fella who holds a grudge.''

Cy shook his head again, more vehemently this time. ''I swear I didn't do it, Marshal. I didn't follow you out of the baggage car. You can ask any of the other jockeys.''

''What about one of *them*? There were a few of 'em who sided you and got knocked around for their trouble.''

''No, it couldn't have been any of us. We all stayed in the baggage car and started up the poker game again. You can ask 'em.''

Longarm grunted. ''You saying they wouldn't shade the truth a mite to protect you?''

''Some of those guys aren't *that* friendly with me. In fact, some of them might like to see me get into trouble so that I couldn't ride against them for a while.'' Cy's chest inflated with pride. ''I'm a pretty good rider, even if I do say so myself.''

''Maybe. Senator Padgett didn't seem to think so.''

Cy shrugged. ''The senator's new at the racing game. He doesn't always understand how these things go.''

''You can't like the way he treats you sometimes, though.'' Longarm rubbed his jaw. ''I wonder what I'd find out if I was to start looking into your movements in Albuquerque, Cy. I wouldn't mind knowing where you went and who you talked to before that trouble yesterday morning.''

Cy's eyes widened in horror. ''You think I had something to do with that assassination attempt on the senator!'' he burst out.

Longarm didn't think that at all—but he was willing to let Cy believe that he did. *"You* tell *me,''* he said coolly. ''Did you?''

Cy clutched at the sleeve of Longarm's coat. He seemed to be truly afraid now. ''You have to believe me, Marshal! I wouldn't do a thing like that. I couldn't! I didn't have anything to do with that fella who shot at the senator!''

''Keep your voice down,'' snapped Longarm. ''Why should I believe you?''

''Because it's the truth!''

''Gents who like to drink too much and get mixed up in high-stakes poker games have been known to lie too,'' Longarm pointed out. ''What were you doing back there at the Crystal Star? Did you figure to make a bet against Caesar and then throw the race so you could clean up? That'd go a long way toward making it easier to put up with Padgett chewing on your ass like he does.''

Cy was shaking his head so violently that he got dizzy and had to put a hand against the wall of the building to steady himself. ''I would *never* do anything like that,'' he declared. ''Sure, I don't much like the senator, but I give him an honest ride every time.'' He grimaced. ''Maybe I do like to knock back a few and play cards, but that's no crime. I swear, Marshal, you've got me all wrong!''

This had gone on long enough, Longarm decided. ''All right,'' he said curtly. ''I ain't saying that I believe you, but I reckon I can give you the benefit of the doubt . . . for now. You'd damned well better walk the straight and narrow from here on out, though. Stay away from the cards and the booze.''

''I . . . I can do that.'' Cy swallowed hard. ''Are you going to tell Senator Padgett about what happened back there at the saloon?''

''That shootout?'' Longarm shook his head. ''That was just a matter of pure-dee bad luck, I reckon. If those gents hadn't recognized me and grabbed their guns, it wouldn't have happened.''

"I never saw either of them before today. I can swear to that too."

"As for you pulling a gun on me . . ."

Cy licked dry lips as he waited for Longarm to finish.

"We'll keep that between us too."

"Thank you, Marshal. I need this job riding for the senator."

"Like I said, you walk the straight and narrow, and there won't be any more trouble."

"You've got my word on it," vowed Cy.

Longarm figured he meant the pledge. If Cy had been telling the truth about everything that had happened, and if he kept his word about not causing any more ruckuses, then that would be one less distraction for Longarm, one less false trail to follow.

But Cy could have been telling the truth about everything else and *still* not be completely innocent. Longarm was going to have to keep that in mind.

"Come on," he said gruffly. "Let's get back to the hotel. You and me both have things to do."

Longarm made one stop along the way, at the store where he had seen a hat like the one he'd lost displayed in the window. Since he hadn't managed to play a single hand in that poker game before all hell broke loose, he still had his expense money. He spent some of it and came out of the store feeling fully dressed again, the Stetson sitting squarely on his head. It would take a few days for it to adjust to his head and fit perfectly, but Longarm already felt a lot better.

He had let Cy go on to the hotel alone. Though the jockey wasn't cleared in Longarm's mind, he was no longer a prime suspect either.

Which was unfortunate in a way, because it left Longarm right back where he had started the day before.

There was nothing like nearly getting shot to give a man an appetite, Longarm mused as he entered the hotel. He went through the lobby and turned right into the dining room, which was beginning to get busy with the lunch crowd. Longarm planned to sit at a stool along the counter, but a female voice called, "Custis! Over here, darling!"

Longarm saw Janice and Julie Cassidy sitting at a table. Janice was the one who had called out to him, and as he ambled up to the table, Julie gave her sister a long look and repeated coolly, "Darling?"

"Well, he is, don't you think?" demanded Janice.

Julie gave Longarm a sultry smile. "I certainly do. You'll join us, won't you, Marshal?"

Longarm took off his new hat and hung it on the back of the chair he pulled out from the table. "Like I said before, I never turn down an invitation from a pair of beautiful ladies."

Janice leaned closer to him and said quietly, "Then you'll come to our room this evening after dinner. It's on the third floor. Number Twelve."

Longarm looked from sister to sister. When his gaze met Julie's, she nodded almost imperceptibly. Longarm scraped a thumbnail along the line of his jaw and sat back in the chair. "That's a mighty nice suggestion, ladies, but I'm afraid I'll have to think on it."

"You do that, Custis," said Janice. "You think on it."

"Think long and hard," Julie said.

Longarm swallowed, unsure what to say next or even whether or not he could get his mouth working properly again. He was saved from the necessity of an immediate reply by the hand that fell on his shoulder and the bluff, hearty voice that said, "There you are, Marshal! I was wondering what had happened to you. I see these lovely young ladies have stolen you away from me again."

Longarm looked up at Senator Miles Padgett. He grinned and said, "They're sort of what you'd call an irresistible force, Senator."

"And we poor men are hardly immovable objects." Padgett reached for one of the empty chairs at the table. "Mind if I join you?"

"By all means, please do," said Janice. "We can talk about the race."

Padgett sat down. A waiter appeared, and the senator ordered a bottle of wine.

The meal passed pleasantly, with most of the discussion concerning the race that would be run in a couple of days. While there was a definite edge of rivalry between the senator and the Cassidy sisters, they got along well.

After a while, Longarm asked Padgett where his assistant was. Padgett laughed and said, "He's still up in the room working. Only Leon would be writing a speech for a session of Congress that won't even convene for a couple of months yet!"

"Sounds like another dedicated federal employee," Longarm said. "Shoot, I think Billy Vail'd be thrilled if I'd think two days ahead, let alone two months."

"There's something to be said for living for the moment," Janice commented. "Wouldn't you say so, Julie?"

"Oh, definitely. The pleasures of the moment shouldn't be underestimated. We don't have any way of knowing what tomorrow's going to bring."

Longarm wasn't in much of a mood for philosophy. He was more interested in the cups of coffee and the decanter of brandy that the waiter brought to the table to finish up the meal.

The Cassidy sisters excused themselves, Janice saying, "We'll leave you men here to smoke cigars and tell bawdy stories."

"We're in the middle of a public dining room, my dear," Padgett said as he and Longarm stood up. "It wouldn't be very proper for the marshal and me to tell bawdy stories in such a place, now would it?"

"All right," Janice said with her dazzling smile. "You can just think about them instead."

Longarm knew what he was thinking about: He was remembering the invitation to join Janice and Julie in their room that evening. As if to reinforce that image in his mind, Julie paused beside him as the sisters left the table. "Don't forget what we were talking about earlier," she said softly to him.

"Not very likely, ma'am," Longarm assured her.

When the Cassidy sisters were gone and Longarm and Padgett had settled back down in their seats to smoke and finish off the brandy, the senator shifted his cigar from one side of his mouth to the other and said, "What was that about?"

"What was what about?" Longarm asked blandly.

"What Julie said about you not forgetting what you talked about earlier."

Longarm shook his head. "Nothing important. They want to buy me a drink at the clubhouse after the race."

"Oh." Padgett seemed rather disappointed. "I thought you might be making some romantic progress with one of the ladies . . . or perhaps both of them."

"I don't need to remind you, Senator, that a gentleman doesn't discuss such things."

"Of course not. Are you a Southerner, Marshal Long?"

"I came out to the frontier from West-by-God Virginia so long ago that I consider myself a Westerner more than anything else," Longarm replied honestly. "I fought in the Late Unpleasantness when I was just a pup, but that was so long ago too that I sort of disremember which side I was on."

Padgett laughed. "A splendid answer. Have you ever given any consideration to a career in politics?"

Longarm had to suppress a shudder at the very thought. "No offense, Senator—but Lord, no! I can't even please one boss most of the time, let alone a whole damned constituency of 'em."

"Well, if you ever change your mind, look me up. I think you'd make an excellent representative for the great state of Colorado."

Longarm tried to picture himself in the halls of Congress. He squinted hard, but he couldn't quite see it. Still, he said politely, "I'll remember that, Senator."

Around mid-afternoon, Longarm, Padgett, and Leon Mercer rode back out to the racetrack to watch Cy putting Caesar through another workout. As the big horse galloped easily around the oval track, Padgett watched raptly. The senator seemed to really enjoy being an owner. Longarm wondered how long that would last before Padgett tired of it. That would depend to a certain extent on how well Caesar did, Longarm decided. He couldn't see Padgett sticking with a loser.

There had been no more attempts on Padgett's life, which came as no surprise to Longarm. He followed Padgett and Mercer back to the paddock, where Caesar was being brushed and rubbed down by his trainer, a wiry old Irishman named O'Malley. Padgett snapped a series of questions about Caesar's condition and performance at Cy, who seemed nervous as he answered them. The jockey kept glancing at Longarm. Not wanting Padgett to suspect there was anything unusual going on between Longarm and Cy, the big lawman eased back into the long building.

He spotted the door to a room where he had seen jockeys going in and out several times. When he tried the knob, it was unlocked. Opening the door slightly, Longarm called, "Anybody home?"

No answer came back.

He slipped into the room and closed the door behind him. Just as he had thought, he was in the room where the jockeys changed into their silks and stored their gear. There were separate cubicles along the walls, and he found the one being used by Cy, identifying it by the colors on the silken shirt hanging there along with the white pants. There was a carpetbag on the floor of the open cubicle.

Longarm bent quickly and picked up the bag. If Cy was indeed still up to something, this might be Longarm's chance to discover it—as long as nobody walked in on him. Cy's traveling bag was back at the hotel, Longarm supposed, so this carpetbag would contain gear relating to the race.

He opened the bag and delved into it, finding a spare set of silks, a pair of riding boots, some gloves, and some cloth-covered weights that gave the bag a surprising amount of heft. Those were the weights that Cy would slip into the pouches on Caesar's saddle to even things up if some of the other jockeys were heavier than he was. Longarm knew there was some method of determining how much weight each of the horses was supposed to carry during the race, but he had never learned what it was.

At the sound of footsteps just outside the door of the jockeys' room, Longarm dropped the square weights back into Cy's bag and closed it up. He put it back where he had found it, then stepped out of the cubicle. When the door into the room opened, he was standing in the center of the floor, lighting a fresh cheroot.

"Oh, there you are, Marshal," Leon Mercer said. "The senator and I wondered where you'd gotten off to."

"Just came in here for a smoke," said Longarm. He dropped his voice conspiratorially. "Just between you and me, Leon, I'm getting a mite tired of the smell of horseshit."

Mercer frowned. "That's too bad," he snapped. "Your job is to protect the senator, not to stop and sniff posies."

That was quite an outburst, considering Mercer's mild nature. Longarm put the cheroot back in his mouth and puffed on it to hide the grin that passed across his face. "You're absolutely right, Leon," he said. "I'd better get back to work."

Padgett didn't question him about his whereabouts when Longarm rejoined him. The three of them went back to the hired buggy and Longarm drove it to the hotel.

Dinner that evening was shared with Padgett and Leon Mercer, and it wasn't nearly as enjoyable as lunch had been. Having ol' Leon for company just wasn't the same as the Cassidy sisters, Longarm reflected. Janice and Julie weren't in the dining room, and he wondered if they were eating in their room upstairs. On the third floor, they'd said. Room Number Twelve.

Longarm couldn't quite get that thought out of his mind.

After dinner, Senator Padgett spent a couple of hours in the lobby talking politics with several other men, some of them guests in the hotel, others local men who came there to pass the evening in stimulating discussion. The talk wasn't that stimulating to Longarm, however. He knew that such things as grain futures and government regulations were important, at least in the long run, but their immediate impact on a fella like him didn't add up to a hill of beans. Still, he sat in a wing-back chair next to Padgett and tried not to yawn overmuch as the senator discoursed on such matters.

Finally, after what seemed like a longer time than it really was, Padgett went up to bed, trailed by Longarm and Mercer. Longarm made sure the senator locked his door to the hall; the connecting door between the rooms was left open. Longarm took off his boots, coat, vest, and tie, draped his gunbelt over the head of the bed, then stretched out on top of the covers in his shirt, trousers, and socks. He waited until the stentorian snores from the other room told him that Padgett was sound asleep.

The senator was as safe here as if he'd been in his own house in Washington. Longarm was sure of that. And though some might call it neglecting his duty to slip out and pay a visit to the Cassidy sisters . . . those who would condemn him for doing so had probably never had two such lovely young women waiting for them. He pulled his boots on, eased out into the hall, and locked the door of his room behind him.

The door of Room Twelve opened almost instantly when he rapped lightly on it. "Custis!" Janice exclaimed happily. "We thought you'd never get here! We were worried that you had decided not to come."

"Just had to wait until the time was right," Longarm said with a grin as he stepped into the room. Janice closed the door behind him.

She was breathtaking, he thought as she moved around him so that he could get a good look at her in the soft light coming from a turned-down lamp. She wore a gown of gossamer lace and blue silk. The neck plunged low enough so that he could see nearly all of the valley between her plump, creamy breasts. Her nipples were erect and stood out urgently against the silk.

Julie was lying on the huge four-poster bed, propped up on a pile of pillows, an equally lovely vision in a gown that was identical except for its color. Julie's outfit was red. Longarm looked from one to the other of them and said to the one in blue, "You *are* Janice, aren't you?"

Both sisters laughed. "Does it really matter?" said the one in red.

"Well . . ."

"I'm Janice," the twin in blue said. "You should be ashamed of yourself, Julie. We don't want to confuse poor Custis."

No man who ever found himself with bounty like this could be called poor, thought Longarm. Janice stepped forward, and his arms came up instinctively to pull her into an embrace. Her head tilted back, and her lush red lips parted invitingly.

Longarm was about to kiss her, but then he paused and looked at Julie. She smiled and said, "Go ahead. I'll just watch for a while."

Longarm had to chuckle and say, "Lordy!" He usually took his loving one at a time, but he supposed in a circumstance like this . . .

Janice's lips pressed hotly against his mouth. He didn't say anything else for a while.

Her body was as soft and warm and intoxicating as he had expected it to be as she pressed against him. The encounters he'd had with each sister had been mighty pleasurable, but the circumstances had forced all three of them to hold back somewhat. He sensed there would be no holding back tonight, none at all.

The kiss finally ended, and Janice stepped back out of his arms. Julie swung her long legs out of the bed and stood up. "My turn," she said, swaying toward him seductively. She looped her arms around his neck and pulled his mouth down to hers.

If anything, her lips and tongue were hotter and wetter than her sister's had been. Longarm's shaft was achingly hard by now, throbbing with the need to be released from the tight confines of his trousers. The Cassidy sisters weren't done tormenting him yet, however.

But it was mighty sweet torture, Longarm thought.

Julie stepped back and stood side by side with Janice. Both of the women slid the straps of their gowns off their shoulders and let the silky garments slide down over their smooth young bodies. The gowns fell in crumpled heaps around their feet. They stood gorgeously, gloriously—and identically—nude before him.

Well, maybe not quite identically, Longarm discovered as his gaze played hungrily over them. He lifted an eyebrow in surprise. Sure enough, he *could* tell the difference between the two of them. Janice's breasts were full and round, crowned with large coral nipples. Julie was slightly less endowed, and her breasts were pear-shaped. Her nipples were smaller and darker but just as erect as her sister's. Longarm's eyes dropped lower, comparing creamy bellies. Janice's was slightly softer, he judged, but Julie worked with the horses and got more exercise, so that was only logical. That brought him to the triangles of fine-spun blond hair at the juncture of their thighs. He cleared his throat and said, ''Ah, I reckon if you wanted me to compare, I've spotted a few differences so far, but . . .''

''Oh, we're not *exactly* alike anywhere,'' Julie said.

''But it takes a very close examination to spot some of the differences,'' added Janice.

Longarm grinned. ''Well, then, I reckon I'd better keep investigating.''

They came toward him, Janice's breasts bobbing a little, Julie's firmer. Each of them took one of his hands. ''There'll be time for that later,'' Julie said, ''after we get you out of these clothes.''

They began undressing him, and the flawless way they worked together told Longarm they had done this before. Julie opened the buttons of his shirt and peeled it back, then twined her fingers in the thick mat of hair on his chest and lowered her lips to one of his nipples. At the same time, Janice slid his trousers down over his hips, and his shaft finally sprang free. She took his manhood in her hand, caressing it in a pumping motion that set Longarm to quivering all over.

''Come on,'' Julie whispered. ''Let's get to bed.''

That sounded like a mighty fine idea to Longarm.

Chapter 9

There was one thing to be said for those Cassidy girls, Longarm told himself later.

They were sure as hell inventive.

Over the next few hours, the three of them coupled in just about every way they conceivably could. Janice and Julie caressed each other a little in the process, but mostly they devoted their attentions to Longarm. At one point, he found himself flat on his back while Janice rode gasping in ecstasy on his burgeoning pole. At the same time, Julie straddled his head so that his tongue could probe the hot, wet folds of her feminine flesh. She let out muffled half-screams as Longarm worked his magic on her. While he was doing that, Janice's hips pumped harder and harder until he could no longer hold back his climax. He emptied himself into her in long, throbbing spurts as her sister reached down and grabbed his head so that she could grind her mound against his face.

A man could die mighty happy this way, Longarm decided.

Finally there was no way any of them could continue, so they lay there cuddled together in a tangle of sheets and sweat-sheened flesh. Each of the sisters had a soft thigh flung over Longarm's legs. He put his arms around them and fondled a breast with each hand. He recalled hearing a fella use the phrase "an embarrassment of riches" one time, and now Longarm surely knew what that gent was talking about. He heaved a long sigh.

"That was heavenly, Custis," Julie said after echoing his sigh. "We'll have to do it again."

Longarm let out a groan.

Julie laughed. "I didn't mean right now," she assured him.

Janice reached down and let her long fingernails trail through the tangle of dark brown hair at his groin. "Do you think Senator Padgett is in such danger that you'll have to travel with us all the way to Denver?"

Longarm frowned a little and asked, "Who said the senator was in danger? I reckon that's why I'm along, to keep any trouble from cropping up."

"Well, that's what I mean, of course," Janice said. "And you seem to be doing an excellent job."

Longarm shrugged awkwardly, considering his position. His shoulders nudged a breast on either side of him. "I'll stay with the senator until my boss tells me to do otherwise."

"Good!" Julie said. "That means we'll have more opportunities to do things like this."

Her fingers closed around his shaft, which he had been certain would be dormant for a while longer. To his surprise—and to the delight of Julie and Janice—it began thickening and lengthening again, the heat of Julie's caress making his manhood grow the way the warmth of the sun touched the seeds in the ground and brought forth wildflowers.

As it turned out, Longarm didn't get back to his own room until nearly dawn. Senator Padgett was still snoring next door. Longarm stripped off his clothes, fell facedown in the bed, and let oblivion claim him.

* * *

Matador, owned by the Cassidy sisters, finished second in the El Paso race, and Senator Padgett's Caesar finished third. The third-place finish was enough to placate the senator somewhat, although he made it plain in his remarks to Cy and O'Malley after the race that he expected to *win* at least once before they reached the end of the circuit. For their part, Janice and Julie were thrilled that Matador had come in second. When Longarm visited with them right after the race, both young women kissed him soundly in their excitement.

"If Matador can just win a couple of races," Julie said, "we'll have enough money to make the improvements we want to make on the farm."

"We'll have a start," corrected Janice. "It's going to take a lot of money to put the place back the way it used to be when Papa was alive."

During the past couple of days, Longarm had spent as much time as he could with the Cassidy sisters and had learned how their father had established the horse farm in Missouri and how their mother had died when the girls were young. Janice had gone away to a fancy finishing school back East, while Julie had stayed on the farm to help their father run it. Things had gone downhill after he'd been kicked in the head by a balky mare and died shortly thereafter from the injury. Janice had returned from school to run the business end of the operation while Julie continued working with the horses. But they'd had a tough time making a go of it. Matador was the best colt they'd had so far, as well as their best hope of getting the farm back on its feet financially. Longarm wished them luck. If it came down to a close finish between Matador and Caesar, he was going to root for Matador. Padgett didn't really need the prize money, at least as far as Longarm knew.

By nightfall, the owners, trainers, jockeys, and horses were all on a westbound train rolling across the desolate landscape of southern New Mexico, heading for Arizona and the racing circuit's next stop in Tucson. The Apache Stakes, Senator Padgett called the race that evening as he and Longarm and Leon Mercer sat in the club car. Padgett had a glass of whiskey in his hand.

"I've heard of Apaches staking folks out, but it didn't have anything to do with horse racing," Longarm said dryly.

Padgett chuckled. "No, I imagine not. The only torture at this race will be waiting to see whether or not Caesar actually wins for a change." A frown replaced the jocular expression on the senator's beefy face. "If he doesn't, I may have to give some thought to finding a new rider."

It was typical of Padgett to place all the blame for Caesar's showing in the races on Cy. The man wasn't about to admit, even to himself, that the other horses might just be faster.

Padgett looked at Longarm and changed the subject by saying quietly, "It's been several days now, and there haven't been any more attempts on my life. When we get to Tucson, don't you think you should wire Marshal Vail and see if he wants you to continue with this assignment?"

Longarm shrugged. "I'll be checking in with Billy anyway. If he wants to pull me off this job, he'll tell me."

"I'm convinced that man in Albuquerque was simply demented. Obviously he hasn't followed us."

It was true enough that the few days in El Paso had passed quite peacefully, with the exception of the gunfight in the Crystal Star saloon—but Padgett didn't know anything about that. It hadn't had anything to do with the assassination attempt in Albuquerque.

While it was true that Padgett was probably in no danger of anyone taking a shot at him, Longarm wasn't ready to give up yet on the job that had brought him here. There were still things to learn, and he intended to dig them out. He knew Billy Vail would agree with him.

Longarm had been able to get together intimately with Janice and Julie Cassidy once more while they were in El Paso, but there was no opportunity to do so on the train. It arrived in Tucson around the middle of the next day, and as had happened before, Padgett, the Cassidy sisters, and the other owners went first to the racetrack to make sure their horses were safely delivered to the stables. After that, it was back to the hotel where the parties were staying.

Tucson was still more of a frontier town than El Paso, though not as boisterous as its neighbor to the southeast, Tombstone. Longarm had been there many times before and knew about the settlement's remaining rough edges. If there *was* going to be trouble, Tucson would be a good place for it to happen. He would have to keep his eyes open and be extra alert.

The hotel was one of the few frame buildings in town. Nearly every structure was made of adobe bricks left their natural color, so the overall effect from a distance was one of the buildings blending into the ground. The hotel rose two stories, with a false third floor on the front, which made it stand out even more from the squat, square buildings around it. The lumber to build the hotel had been hauled in by wagons from the heavily timbered slopes of the mountains that rose in the distance. Those pines had also furnished the planks that had been used to build the grandstands around the racetrack. Like many things in Tucson, the track and the stands were spanking new. There had been a settlement here for many years, ever since Spanish explorers in search of treasure had come through the area and founded the original town. None of the walls from the Spanish settlement still stood, but its influence continued to be felt. There was a sleepiness, a lassitude, in the hot midday air that practically cried out for a *siesta*.

Senator Padgett wasn't particularly interested in a nap, however. He said to Longarm as they entered the hotel, "I want to see one of those Mexican cantinas. I've heard about them, but I've never seen one for myself."

"I'm not certain that would be a good idea, Senator," Leon Mercer said from behind them. "I've heard that such places can be rather, ah, dangerous."

Padgett turned to the aide with a disgusted look. "That's why I'm going to take Marshal Long with me," said Padgett, waving the unlit cigar in his hand at Longarm. "You don't have to go if you don't want to, Leon." He paused, then added, "If you're *scared* to go."

There were plenty of times when grown men acted just like little boys, Longarm reflected, and he supposed he was as guilty of that as any other man. He waited to see if Padgett would resort to the infamous double-dog dare to get Mercer to accompany them, but it proved to be unnecessary. Mercer sighed and said, "Very well. I'll go with you. But don't blame me if some . . . some *bandido* sticks a knife in your ribs, Senator!"

Padgett guffawed and slapped Mercer on the back, staggering the smaller man a little. "That's the spirit, Leon! Don't worry, though. Marshal Long won't let anything happen to me."

The senator was a mighty confident hombre, thought Longarm. He hoped that confidence was well placed as they went in search of a cantina.

At this hour of the day, the settlement was quiet, baking in the heat of the noontime sun. Longarm didn't care much for this impulse of the senator's, but he supposed that if Padgett was bound and determined to visit a cantina, this was as good a time as any. They would be less likely to run into trouble now.

The place Longarm found wasn't far from the hotel. As he and Padgett and Mercer passed through the arched entrance into the cooler dimness of the interior, Longarm paused to let his eyes adjust to the change in light.

This was a typical Southwestern cantina, with tables scattered around the big main room on a hard-packed dirt floor. A bar made of wide planks nailed onto empty barrels ran across part of the rear wall. At the end of the bar was another arched doorway, this one covered with a curtain of beads. The air was heavy with the odors of tobacco smoke, stale beer, tequila, and unwashed human flesh. A couple of men stood at the bar, while three more sat at a table. They were the only customers. A stout Mexican in a dirty white shirt and apron was behind the bar pouring the shots of tequila being downed by the two men standing there. The three men at the table were passing around a bucket of beer. A lush-bodied woman with a mass of curly black hair leaned an elbow against the bar. Her figure was displayed to its best advantage in a low-cut peasant blouse decorated with fancy embroidery and a skirt that hugged her hips before flaring out around her legs. Looking around the place, Longarm thought the word "squalid" came to mind. From the expression on Leon Mercer's face, complete with frown-creased forehead and pursed lips, Mercer agreed. Senator Padgett seemed to be impressed by what he saw, however.

"My God, this is positively . . . earthy," Padgett said. "And so colorful."

Longarm didn't see anything particularly colorful about the cantina. The woman's skirt was bright red, but that was just about the only spot of color he noticed. But there was no point in arguing with Padgett about the matter. Longarm just wanted them to have a drink and then get out of there.

He eyed the customers as he and his two companions crossed the room. He didn't want a repeat of what had happened back in El Paso. The three men at the table were white and looked like cowboys, no doubt from one of the nearby ranches. The pair at the bar wore sombreros and *charro* jackets, and they wore their guns low and tied down. They were bad hombres—or at least thought they were. Longarm didn't recognize either of them, though, so he could at least hope that they didn't know him from somewhere else. And hope, as well, that they wouldn't start shooting at him.

The woman perked up a little as the newcomers approached the bar. "*Hola, señores.* What can Lupe do for you?" She batted her eyelashes in what she obviously considered a seductive manner as she asked the question.

"Tequila," Padgett said, grinning broadly at her. "For me and my friends. No, on second thought, tequila for everyone!"

One of the cowboys at the table called out, "Hey, much obliged, mister! That's mighty generous of you."

"*Muchas gracias,*" said one of the thin-lipped gents at the bar. He gave Padgett a curt nod.

The bartender refilled the glasses of the two Mexicans, then poured drinks for Longarm, Padgett, and Mercer. He finished by pouring three shots for the cowboys and placing the glasses on a tray so that Lupe could carry them over to the table. As she did so, Padgett's eyes followed her swaying hips hungrily.

"A fine-looking woman, wouldn't you say?" he muttered to Longarm. Without waiting for the marshal to respond, he went on. "I've never had a little chile pepper like that. I imagine they're pretty spicy."

His voice was loud enough so that the other two men at the bar might be able to hear it. Longarm said quietly, "I'd be careful about talk like that if I was you. Some folks get a mite touchy."

"Why, I didn't mean any offense." Padgett seemed startled that Longarm would have even suggested such a thing. "Sorry, Marshal. I'll try not to upset the greasers."

Longarm winced. He hadn't particularly wanted it known that he was a lawman, just in case any of the gents in here were on the dodge, and Padgett's comment about "greasers" might just make the situation worse. From the corner of his eye, he saw how the other two men at the bar stiffened. Neither of them had drunk the tequila Padgett had bought for them, and now they pushed the glasses away.

"Pour that out, Pablo," one of them said to the bartender. "We will not drink anything bought by filthy gringo coins."

"Wait just a minute, sir," Padgett said, turning toward the two *charros*. "I've already pointed out that I meant no offense by my comment about the young lady. I was just admiring her beauty."

One of the men spat a curse in Spanish. "Lupe needs no compliments from the likes of you."

The object of the discussion had delivered the drinks to the table. Now she hurried back over to the bar, looking as nervous as the bartender, and said quickly, "There is no need to argue, *mi amigos*. My honor is not insulted."

"A worthless *puta* like you has no honor," snapped one of the Mexicans. "But this dog of a gringo had insulted us by calling us greasers."

Leon Mercer let out a low moan of sheer terror. His drink

was untouched on the bar. Suddenly he snatched up the glass and gulped down the fiery tequila, as if to fortify himself for the trouble he seemed certain was coming.

Longarm also figured things were about to go from bad to worse. He had known that Padgett could be crass and crude at times, and he'd figured that came from being a politician. It had to be difficult to hide your true feelings all the time and only tell people what you thought they wanted to hear. But he had certainly never expected the senator to come in here and provoke trouble so quickly and effortlessly. It was almost like Padgett *wanted* to start a fight. . . .

That thought could have done with some more pondering, but there was no time for it. The untouched drinks still sat in front of the two Mexicans, and Padgett pointed at them as he said loudly, "Now *I'm* going to be insulted if you don't drink those. There's nothing wrong with them, and where I come from a man doesn't dishonor another man by turning down a drink."

"What does a dog know of honor?"

Longarm reached for Padgett's arm. It was time for that better part of valor he'd heard tell of. "Come on," he said. "We're going back to the hotel."

Padgett jerked his arm free. "Not yet. Not until these men do something with those drinks."

The two Mexicans did something, all right. They picked up the glasses and splashed the tequila all over the front of Padgett's suit. The senator gaped down at the wet mess in astonishment, then shouted, "By God, I won't stand for that!" He lunged at the nearest of the Mexicans, swinging a fist at the man's head.

Longarm darted forward, trying to get between Padgett and the other men. The senator's fist brushed the side of his head, making his ear sting. Longarm ignored that and lowered his shoulder, driving into the chest of the Mexican and knocking the man back against his companion. Both men went down.

Longarm jerked around and barked, "Get out of here! Now!" at Padgett and Mercer. Mercer was already tugging frantically on the senator's arm, urging him to run.

"Damn it, this is my fight!" protested Padgett.

"Not any more! Now git!"

Longarm didn't have time to continue arguing. One of the Mexicans was back on his feet, and Longarm saw the flicker of a knife in his hand. He ducked back against the bar as the blade lanced out at him like the tongue of a snake. As the Mexican slashed at him again, Longarm grabbed the bottle of tequila that still sat on the bar and used it to block the knife. The blade scraped off the thick glass, then Longarm brought the bottle down hard on the man's wrist. With a yelp of pain, the man dropped the knife.

From the corner of his eye, Longarm saw Mercer prodding the reluctant Padgett out of the cantina and felt a surge of relief. At least the senator wasn't going to get himself killed over some stupid, senseless argument.

Of course, he might not be able to say the same for himself, Longarm realized, because the second *charro* was back on his feet, and the man was reaching for the pistol in that tied-down holster. He was fast too.

Longarm slowed him down a little by flipping the bottle at him. The man had to put up an arm to bat it aside. That gave Longarm the chance to reach his own gun. He palmed out the .44 and brought it up level in one smooth motion. "I wouldn't," he said coldly as the Mexican's hand touched the butt of his gun.

One of the three white cowboys, who had watched the whole fracas from the table, let out a whistle of admiration. "Whoo-eee! That fella's faster on the draw than Marshal Earp down at Tombstone!"

Longarm had never had any interest in being known as a fast gun. He was fast enough on the draw to have stayed alive this long, and that was all he cared about. Now, as the Mexican slowly moved his hand away from his gun, Longarm nodded and said, "I'm obliged to you for seeing the light of reason, old son. Neither one of us has any business dying over what some loudmouthed blowhard has to say."

"You know this *amigo* of yours is—"

"Is damned hard to swallow sometimes," Longarm finished with a nod. "I sure do. And he ain't really my *amigo*. But I have to look out for him anyway."

The two Mexicans exchanged a glance that told Longarm they understood what he meant. It was his job to stand between Padgett and whatever trouble came up, even trouble of the senator's own making, and they could respect him for doing just that. The one who was holding the sore wrist that Longarm had cracked with the bottle rasped, "Do not let him come in here again."

"You don't have to worry about that," Longarm assured him. "I reckon he's had enough local color to last him for a while."

At least, Longarm damned well hoped so.

He holstered his gun, but he kept a close eye on the gents at the bar until he was out of the cantina. Squinting against the bright sunlight, he walked quickly toward the hotel. He was still plenty angry at Padgett for provoking the confrontation, even though no one had been hurt seriously. It was just a matter of luck that no one had gotten killed.

Going straight to the senator's room, Longarm rapped on the door. Mercer opened it almost immediately, as if they had been waiting for him. The pallor on the face of the senator's assistant was even deeper than usual.

"There you are, Marshal," Mercer said. "We were afraid you might have been killed—"

"No thanks to your boss that I wasn't," Longarm snapped as he shouldered past Mercer. The smaller man got out of his way and shut the door behind him. Longarm faced Padgett, who stood near the window smoking a cigar. "What was the idea, Senator? You trying to start a war with Mexico? Or did you just decide it was time to start acting like an asshole?"

Padgett's face darkened redly. "By God, I don't have to take that kind of talk from you, Long!"

"The hell you don't." Longarm's anger got the best of him, and he stepped forward and prodded Padgett in the chest with a finger. "You acted like you wanted to start that fracas, and I want to know why. Maybe you figured that I'd jump in—hell, you had to know I would!—and what you really wanted was to get *me* killed!''

Padgett stared at him, eyes wide with disbelief. ''Why in heaven's name would I want you dead, Marshal?''

Longarm caught himself just in time. He almost blurted out, *Maybe you've finally figured out why I'm really here.* Instead, he said, ''You've made it pretty clear you don't think there's any reason for me to keep riding hard on you.''

''But I'd hardly try to arrange things so that you'd be killed just because of that!''

Longarm had to admit the senator was right: That made a mighty feeble motive. He said, ''You've been a little jealous right from the start of all the attention those Cassidy sisters have been paying me.''

''Good Lord! I'm a married man, Marshal. I couldn't risk my reputation—my very career—by becoming romantically involved with women young enough to be my daughters!''

''Plenty of politicos have done that very thing, and lived to regret it,'' Longarm pointed out.

Padgett looked distinctly uncomfortable. ''Yes, I know, but I . . . I could never do such a thing, Marshal. You see, I . . . I love my wife. I may flirt with other women, but I've never been unfaithful to her.''

He was so obviously embarrassed by the admission that Longarm found himself believing it. Of course, that didn't really change anything, since Longarm could think of only one really good reason for Padgett to want him dead, and the Cassidy sisters had nothing to do with it. Padgett might still be mixed up in that other matter. But there was an equal chance that he was innocent.

''All right,'' Longarm said. ''Sorry I accused you, Senator.''

''I realize I used very poor judgment in my remarks in that cantina—''

''You sure as blazes did,'' Longarm confirmed grimly.

"But I didn't mean anything by any of it. I really didn't."

Again, Longarm found himself believing the politician. That would be a bad habit to get into, he told himself, a downright dangerous habit. He took a deep breath and said, "No harm done. How about one of those cheroots you carry around?"

Padgett smiled and reached for his vest pocket without hesitation. "Of course! There you go, Marshal. I take it that we're, ah, friends again?"

Longarm wasn't aware that they had ever been friends, but it seemed important to Padgett, so he nodded and said, "Sure." Leon Mercer stepped forward and lit the cigar the senator had given Longarm, and after puffing on it for a moment, Longarm asked, "When's the race here in Tucson?"

"Tomorrow," replied Padgett. "Then it's on to Carson City the next day. Our stay here won't be a long one."

Longarm nodded. The circuit was about to swing north; then after a couple of stops it would turn east. He only had a certain amount of time to find out what he wanted to know before it was too late.

Those thoroughbreds, Matador and Caesar and the others, weren't the only ones in a race. Longarm was too.

And the stakes in that match might just turn out to be life and death.

Chapter 10

There were no adjoining rooms in the hotel in Tucson, but Longarm had managed to get three rooms side by side. Senator Padgett was in the middle one, with Longarm and Leon Mercer flanking him. That arrangement was the best Longarm could do without actually bunking with the senator, and he wasn't willing to do that just to keep up appearances. That evening when he turned in, he left Mercer in Padgett's room, the two of them sitting at a table huddled together over a welter of papers. "These are the reports from the banking committee, Senator," Mercer was saying as Longarm stifled a yawn and closed the door.

He went to his own room and glanced at the piece of broken matchstick he had left wedged between the door and the jamb. It was still visible a couple of inches above the floor. Satisfied that no one had gone through the door while he was away from the room, Longarm unlocked it, turned the knob, and stepped inside.

Something came whipping out of the shadows, passing within a couple of inches of his face before it struck the door. His hand was still holding the edge of the door, and he felt the faint shiver of impact through his fingers. Instinct sent him forward and down, diving into the room as he clawed for his gun. As he fell, he saw the thin curtains fluttering in front of the window. That window had been closed when he left, but now it stood open, admitting the night breeze that stirred the curtains. Clearly, it had let in more than a breeze.

Longarm had checked that window earlier and been convinced that no one could climb through it without going to a lot of trouble. There was no balcony outside. But someone had gone to the trouble of getting in that way, and the hombre was still here. Longarm saw his silhouette in front of the window. Flame licked out from the center of that dark shadow as noise filled the room. The sound of the gunshot hammered against Longarm's ears.

He double-actioned the Colt in his hand, adding to the racket as he squeezed off two shots. A heavy grunt came from the dark figure as it was flung backward by the impact of the slugs. The man's shape filled the window for an instant, then was suddenly gone. Longarm heard a soggy thump from the street outside as he scrambled to his feet. He lunged to the window and peered out, saw the sprawled shape in the street below the window.

Someone was pounding a fist against the wall of his room. "Marshal!" Padgett called through the wall. "Marshal Long, are you all right in there?"

"I'm fine," Longarm shouted back. "Stay right there until I get back, Senator!"

Then he turned and hurried out of the room, running down the corridor outside to the staircase. He descended the stairs to the lobby of the hotel in several great bounds. The lobby was empty, but the porch of the hotel seemed to be almost full, he noted through the big glass front windows. As Longarm stepped onto the porch, which was lit by several lanterns hanging from its ceiling, he recognized most of the bystanders as horse owners, trainers, and others connected with the racing circuit, all of whom were staying here at the hotel.

"Step aside there!" he barked. "U.S. marshal coming through."

A path opened in front of Longarm, and he moved to the edge of the narrow porch. The corpse lay right in front of the porch, and enough light spilled on it for Longarm to recognize the man as one of the Mexicans from the fight in the cantina earlier in the day. The man lay on his back, and Longarm could see the dark bloodstains on the front of the white shirt under the *charro* jacket. That was pretty good shooting, he noted, even if he did say so himself.

Longarm stepped down from the porch after checking to make sure the man wasn't still holding a gun. He was fairly certain that the hombre was dead, but he searched for a pulse to verify it. Just as he had thought, there wasn't one. A six-shooter lay several feet away, Longarm noticed, and he figured the Mexican had dropped it there while falling backward through the window in Longarm's room.

"What the bloody blue hell is goin' on here?" demanded a harsh, high-pitched voice.

Longarm looked up and saw a burly figure standing over him. The man wore a tin star pinned to his shirt. "You the town marshal?" Longarm asked.

"Deputy sheriff," grunted the man. "Hey, I started askin' questions first!"

Longarm straightened from his crouch next to the body. "I'm United States Deputy Marshal Custis Long." He nodded toward the corpse. "This fella here just tried to ventilate me up yonder in my hotel room after throwing what I reckon was a knife at my head. He missed both times. I didn't."

"I can see that," the deputy sheriff said. "You got anything provin' you're really who you say you are, mister?"

"Sure." Longarm dug out his identification and handed the folder to the local lawman, who studied the badge and documents intently in the light from the porch. When shadows from the bystanders kept falling over Longarm's papers, the deputy sheriff twisted his thick neck and snapped, "Everybody clear off! The shootin's all over." He glanced back at Longarm and added, "Ain't it?"

"Far as I'm concerned, it is. Unless somebody starts trying to plug me again," Longarm qualified.

The local badge returned Longarm's bona fides as the crowd on the porch began to reluctantly filter back into the hotel. "Name's Bullfincher," said the deputy sheriff. "That fella there on the ground leakin' blood is called Rodriguez. Heard tell he was a pretty bad hombre, but he never caused no real trouble here in town. You know why he'd want to kill you?"

"I had a run-in with him earlier in the day in a cantina," Longarm said. There was no point in trying to hide that fact. Deputy Bullfincher would have likely been able to turn up witnesses to the fight without too much trouble. "He and another fella took offense at something somebody said."

"That other fella'd be his pard Guzman, another bad 'un. What'd you say to set 'em off?"

Longarm shook his head. "Wasn't me. I just stepped in to keep things from getting out of hand."

"From the looks of it, *you're* the one Rodriguez was holdin' a grudge against," Bullfincher pointed out.

"It does look that way," admitted Longarm.

Bullfincher knelt beside the corpse, grunting with the effort of bending his heavyset body. A fast, efficient search of Rodriguez's pockets turned up a clasp knife, cigarette makin's, a few pesos—and a roll of twenty-dollar bills. Bullfincher let out a whistle of surprise. "I've heard rumors that Rodriguez and Guzman hold up stagecoaches from time to time. Reckon this must be some of the loot from one of those jobs."

"Can I take a look at those bills?" asked Longarm.

"Sure, I guess so," Bullfincher replied with a frown. He handed the money to Longarm, who unrolled the bills. There were five of them, all twenties. Longarm looked at them closely, rubbed his fingers lightly over their surface, then passed them back to Bullfincher. "You're right, Deputy," he said. "Must be holdup loot."

Bullfincher tucked the money into his shirt pocket. "I'll take it over to the Wells Fargo office later and turn it over to the agent. Right now, let's go upstairs and take a look at your room."

Longarm didn't argue the point, though he wasn't sure what the deputy sheriff was looking for. They climbed the stairs, ignoring the questions flung at them by the curious folks inside the hotel lobby. As their heavy footsteps echoed along the second-floor corridor, the door of Padgett's room opened a crack and Leon Mercer peered out. Seeing Longarm, Mercer opened the door wider.

"Are you really all right, Marshal?" he asked. "Those shots were so loud, and the senator is quite concerned."

"Senator?" echoed Bullfincher. "You didn't say nothin' about no senator, Marshal."

"Hadn't gotten around to it yet," Longarm said dryly. "Come on, Leon. Bring the senator too."

Padgett and Mercer emerged into the hallway, and Longarm quickly performed introductions. Deputy Bullfincher seemed more impressed to be meeting a United States senator than he had been by Longarm's status as a federal lawman. "You can rest easy, Senator," Bullfincher said. "One of our local badmen tried to settle a score with the marshal here for a run-in in a cantina earlier, but it didn't have nothin' to do with you. Normally Tucson's a nice, quiet little town."

Longarm knew that was hardly the case, but he didn't bother contradicting Bullfincher. Padgett didn't give him a chance to anyway. The senator said, "You're wrong, Deputy. What happened tonight *is* my fault. You see, Marshal Long was protecting *me* when he got in that fight earlier. I provoked it." He added quickly, "Not intentionally, of course."

Bullfincher's bushy eyebrows rose in surprise. "You, Senator? Startin' a fight in a cantina?" His tone made it clear how difficult that was for him to believe.

Padgett winced and said, "Let's not spread that around, shall we? I never dreamed one of those men would come back and . . . and try to kill Marshal Long!"

"You hurt a Mex's pride, he has a hard time gettin' over it," said Bullfincher. He pointed a stubby forefinger at the door of Longarm's room, which still stood open. "Looky there. Rodriguez left you a souvenir, all right."

A dagger with a long, thin blade was still stuck in the door.

Longarm stepped over to it, took hold of the handle, and wrenched the blade free. He handed the weapon to Bullfincher. "You'd better keep it for evidence. I don't need it."

"Yeah, I reckon you're right. If there's ever any question about any o' this, that dagger's proof Rodriguez tried to kill you. We'll hold an inquest tomorrow, but there ain't no doubt in my mind the jury'll make a findin' of self-defense."

"The inquest will have to be tomorrow morning, Deputy," Padgett said. "There's a horse race tomorrow afternoon. That's why we're all here."

"Shoot, yeah, we can do it in the mornin', I reckon. Ten o'clock all right?"

Longarm nodded.

"Well, I better see about havin' that body hauled off," Bullfincher said with a sigh. "And you best sleep with one eye open, Marshal Long. If Rodriguez was gunnin' for you, chances are Guzman is too."

"We'll all be careful, Deputy," Padgett said. "Thank you."

Bullfincher shuffled off. Leon Mercer rubbed a hand over his face and said in a low voice, "Dear Lord, what's going to happen *next*?"

"Nothing, I hope," said Longarm. "I want to get some sleep."

"But how can you sleep knowing that somewhere out there a man may well want to kill you?"

"Leon, old son, I reckon there hasn't been a night pass since I pinned on a law badge when somebody, somewhere, hasn't wanted to see me dead."

"Well, you can be nonchalant if you like," Mercer said with a sniff, "but I know that *I* don't intend to close my eyes this entire night."

"Come on, Leon," Padgett said, putting a hand on his assistant's shoulder. "I never thought that *I'd* be the one saying this, but we still have work to do."

"You're right, of course, Senator. . . ."

The two of them disappeared back into Padgett's room. Longarm went into his own room, closing and locking the door behind him. He blew out the lamp so he wouldn't be silhouetted. Then a quick look out the window told him how Rodriguez had gotten into the room. A knotted lasso hung out there, leading up to the false third floor. Rodriguez had climbed onto the roof, tied the rope onto something, placed it through the window above Longarm's in the building's false front, and climbed down hand over hand. Longarm took his own folding knife from his pocket, opened it, and cut the rope as high up as he could reach. Then he closed the window, took off his boots, coat, vest, and tie, and stretched out on the bed. He had seen Janice and Julie Cassidy in the crowd downstairs and had met their eyes long enough to assure them that he was all right. He hoped they wouldn't wait until later and then show up at his door expecting a few hours of romping. Not that such a prospect wouldn't be delightful—most of the time. Tonight, though, Longarm wanted to think.

He would have sworn that the bad blood between him and the two Mexicans had been put aside following the fight in the cantina. At least, enough so that Rodriguez shouldn't have been lurking in his hotel room waiting to ambush him.

But there was nothing saying that Rodriguez couldn't have had *another* reason for trying to kill him. An even better reason. A hundred better reasons, come to think of it, because while Longarm was willing to let Deputy Bullfincher believe that the money Rodriguez had been carrying had come from a stagecoach holdup, Longarm didn't think that was the case at all. It was blood money, paid for *his* blood. He was certain of it. The bills had told him something else too.

For the first time, he was absolutely sure that his hunch had been correct. He was on the right trail.

And from here on out, it would probably just get more perilous.

• • •

As Deputy Bullfincher had predicted, the coroner's jury found that Longarm had acted in self-defense in the killing of Rodriguez, and they stopped just short of congratulating him for a job well done.

Longarm headed for the racetrack as soon as the inquest was concluded. Senator Padgett was anxious to get out there and see how preparations for the race were going. Cy had put Caesar through some practice runs early that morning, and O'Malley reported that the times had been good. "The track's fast today, Senator," the Irishman said. " 'Tis a good feelin' I be havin' about this race."

"I hope you're right," Padgett said. "I'm ready to win one for a change."

Longarm found himself cornered in the paddock by Janice and Julie. "What in the world happened last night?" Janice demanded. "We heard a lot of shooting, and everyone said that you were involved."

"They said you killed a man," added Julie.

"I'm afraid that's right," Longarm said. "Didn't have much choice in the matter. He was trying to kill me at the time."

Janice shuddered. "I'm getting a little tired of the West. It's so violent out here!"

"It can be," admitted Longarm. "A lot of people are working to make it less dangerous, though."

"Including you," said Julie. Longarm acknowledged the comment with a nod and a half-shrug.

Janice linked her arm with his. "I'll be glad when we reach Denver. At least it's a civilized town!"

Longarm didn't bother mentioning all the times he had come too damned close to getting killed right there inside the city limits of Denver. If Janice wanted to believe it was a civilized place, then so be it. He was more concerned at the moment with the way her breast was pressing softly and warmly against his arm. Julie took his other arm and leaned into it. "Walk us to Matador's stall," Julie said.

"My pleasure, ladies."

And it was, just as it was his pleasure to eat lunch with them in the clubhouse a little later. Senator Padgett and

Leon Mercer joined them, of course, as did the other own-ers. Longarm had met all of the other men at least briefly during the trip; Janice and Julie were the only females on the racing circuit this time around. For the rest of the day, Longarm paid more attention to the other owners, watching them closely, engaging them in idle conversation. They were a diverse group, as might have been expected. Three of the men were from Texas, two each from Louisiana and Kansas, and one apiece from Arkansas, Iowa, and Ken-tucky. Senator Padgett's home state of Colorado was the farthest west of any man's in the bunch. That didn't sur-prise Longarm. Western horses were bred more for short, fast bursts of speed as they worked cattle, so that was what Westerners knew best. The long-legged thoroughbreds that ran the longer distances came mostly from the South and East, although like everything else in the country, they were spreading west.

By and large, the owners were a friendly group and got along well despite the natural rivalries. Longarm didn't sense any real bitterness among them, certainly nothing that would lead to violence. Of course, he wasn't expecting to find anything of that nature. He was on the trail of cold-blooded greed, rather than hot-blooded anger.

As he watched the race later that afternoon from Pad-gett's box, Longarm began to worry that the senator would have a fit of apoplexy and fall down dead. Padgett was that excited as he jumped up and down, screaming and red-faced, while the horses swept around and around the track and Caesar gradually pulled ahead of the others. Longarm was no expert, but as far as he could tell, Cy was riding the ride of his life, doing everything right and not making a single wrong move. By the time the horses began flashing across the finish line, Caesar was a full three lengths ahead, the clear winner.

Padgett whooped and embraced Leon Mercer, jerking the smaller man off his feet in his exuberance. "We won, Leon, we won!" shouted Padgett.

"Indeed we . . . did, sir," Mercer gasped. "I'm sorry, sir, but I . . . can't breathe!"

Padgett released his assistant and turned to Longarm, who stopped him by holding up a hand. "I'm happy for you, old son, but don't even think it," Longarm warned.

"All right, but I'm buying all the drinks!"

Longarm grinned. "I got no problem with that."

The three of them began making their way down toward the winner's circle. Longarm also wanted to find the Cassidy sisters and congratulate them on Matador's third-place finish. He knew they needed some wins in order to accumulate enough prize money to get their ranch back on its feet, but at least they had finished in the money in this race.

As he had been doing all day, Longarm kept an eye out for Guzman, the other Mexican from the cantina. Deputy Bullfincher had been convinced that Guzman would be gunning for him too. Longarm wasn't quite so sure. Rodriguez had been paid to bushwhack him, but that didn't mean Guzman had been too. Even if the person who wanted Longarm dead had enlisted Guzman in the effort, Guzman had surely seen what had happened to Rodriguez. Guzman could have returned the money to his erstwhile employer—or else kept it and pulled a double cross by taking off for the tall and uncut. Either way, Longarm didn't think he had to worry overmuch about Guzman, but he still didn't intend to take any foolish chances.

When they reached the winner's circle, Padgett grabbed Cy and O'Malley both, hugging the jockey and the trainer in turn. "God, I've never been so thrilled in my whole life!" he said. "When Caesar reached the finish line, I thought I was going to die from the excitement!"

"We all did, Senator," Mercer said dryly.

Several of the other owners arrived to pump Padgett's hand and slap his back in congratulation, so Longarm took advantage of the opportunity to slip away and find the Cassidy sisters. They looked excited at Matador's finish, but nevertheless somewhat disappointed.

"I really thought he'd win today," Julie said as she stroked the shoulder of the big chestnut. Matador was sweating and his sides were still heaving from the exertion of the race.

"I reckon it was just Caesar's day," said Longarm, knowing the words were scant comfort. "You'll get 'em next time."

"I hope so," Janice said with a sigh. "Coming on this trip was expensive, you know. If we don't go home with a sizable amount of money, we won't be able to cover our expenses and make the necessary repairs to the ranch."

Longarm shook his head. "Wish I could help you, ladies, but I don't know a damned thing about this kind of horse racing. And on what Uncle Sam pays me, I can't loan anybody more than whiskey-and-cigar money."

Both of the young women looked alarmed. "Please, Custis, don't think we were hinting for any such thing!" Janice said.

"We can take care of ourselves," Julie said.

Janice took one of Longarm's hands in both of hers. "We're just glad you've been along for most of the trip, Custis, because having you for a friend has meant so much to us."

"It's been my pleasure, ma'am. And I mean that."

Janice smiled up at him and practically purred, "It's been our pleasure too. Quite a few times, in fact."

Longarm had to grin at her boldness.

The aftermath of the race passed without incident, as did that night at the hotel. The next westbound train would pass through Tucson the following morning, and the circuit would continue. Though there were no races scheduled for California, the route of the group would take them through the eastern part of that state, following the rail line as it curved north and made connections with the Union Pacific Railroad, which would take them to Carson City and Reno. Several days of travel would be involved, Longarm knew. He didn't mind. He didn't expect anything to happen while they were on the train—although he would not have ruled out the possibility of another attempt on his life—and the interval would give him time to ponder everything that had happened. A couple of theories had started to take shape in his mind, and he wanted to test them out by taking every fact he could think of and holding it up to scrutiny.

He went to sleep that night thinking about the case, and dreamed about clues that proved too elusive for him to grasp.

Mountains and deserts had a bleak, spectacular beauty to them for the most part, Longarm had learned over the years, but such landscapes got mighty old and tiresome after a few miles, especially when they were viewed from the window of a moving train. It wasn't like riding horseback through such terrain, when you were moving slowly enough to appreciate all the subtle differences. When he had to do too much traveling by rail, he usually wound up sitting as far back in his seat as he could, hat tipped down over his eyes, an unlit cheroot clenched in his teeth. That was the position in which he found himself a couple of days after leaving Tucson. It would be another day and a half before the group of travelers arrived in Carson City for the next race.

Longarm had done his pondering, then gone through it all again and yet again. He had ideas, but no proof of anything. As darkness settled down on the train while it rolled through the Southwestern landscape, he decided that the time had come to do a little more snooping around.

First, though, he would have to wait until everyone was asleep. He straightened from his half-reclined position, frowning at the twinge in his lower back from stiff muscles, as Senator Padgett announced that he and Mercer were going to the club car for dinner. "I'll come with you," Longarm said, placing his hands on his knees and pushing himself to his feet.

"We could bring something back for you if you'd like, Marshal," Padgett offered. "Don't feel as if you have to tag along behind me everywhere I go. I think we've pretty well established by now that any threat to me is over." Padgett snorted. "I don't know why Chief Marshal Vail didn't relieve you of this job when you wired him while we were in Tucson."

"I reckon Billy's got his reasons," Longarm said.

The main one being that Longarm hadn't asked to be relieved, didn't want to be relieved. This assignment wasn't over yet, not by a long shot, and Longarm and Billy both knew it. In fact, if everything worked out the way Longarm hoped, it was about to start heating up again.

Janice and Julie Cassidy were already in the club car, and they insisted that Longarm, Padgett, and Mercer join them, which the three men did without hesitation. Dinner passed pleasantly, and when it was over, Julie seized a moment alone with Longarm to say quietly, "I hope you'll come to see us tonight after everyone else is asleep, Custis."

It was a mighty tempting invitation, the kind that any man, including Longarm, would have been thrilled to receive. But there was something else he had in mind to do first. Maybe if that other business didn't take too long, he could stop by the sisters' compartment. . . .

"I'll see what I can do, Miss Julie," he promised, hoping they wouldn't be too disappointed if they had to wait a while. Hoping too that he would still feel like seeing them when he finished his other errand.

The prospect of bedding the Misses Cassidy again only added to the anticipation that kept Longarm on edge all evening. He concealed what he was feeling as best he could, but he was greatly relieved when Padgett and Mercer finally turned in. Sitting just outside the compartment, as was his habit, he waited until he hadn't heard any noise coming from inside for nearly half an hour, except for Padgett's usual snoring.

Longarm stood up then and began making his way back along the train toward the baggage car.

The car was dark and deserted when he got there, as he had hoped it would be. He had overheard enough conversation among the jockeys the past few days to know that their running poker game had moved to the caboose and expanded to include the train's brakemen and conductor. That was a lucky break for him, and he was going to take advantage of it. He dug out a lucifer from his coat pocket, flicked it into life with an iron-hard thumbnail, and lit one of the lanterns hanging on the wall of the car. That gave him enough light to begin his search.

He proceeded methodically. This was hardly the first search Longarm had conducted. He went through the trunks and the carpetbags and the valises, opening even those that were locked without much trouble. His keen, experienced eye scanned the contents of each item. He took care not to disturb things so much that it would be readily apparent a search had taken place.

His disappointment grew as he went through more than half the baggage without finding a thing suspicious or even very strange. There were plenty of clothes, both clean and dirty, and a handful of books, both clean and dirty. Racing silks, extra tack, bottles of liniment good for both man and horse. Toys, corsets, suspenders, baby bottles, birdcages, sheet music, hats, cosmetics, tools, musical instruments, stuffed and mounted fish . . . this baggage car·contained all the odds and ends to be expected that might belong to a whole trainload of passengers.

But so far, not what he was looking for.

He came to the bags belonging to Senator Padgett, recognizing them from all the times he had seen them carried in and out of various hotels. Having spent most of his time with Padgett, he knew the senator about as well as anyone on this train. Knew him well enough, in fact, that it was doubly important he go through the man's baggage, Longarm thought. He opened a valise and began looking at the contents by the light of the lantern hanging behind him.

It took only a moment for Longarm to find one of the things he had been searching for.

The false bottom of the valise had never been meant to hide anything from a diligent professional. Longarm felt the hidden catch in the lining and quickly emptied the valise of its innocuous contents. Then he worked the catch and lifted the false bottom.

Six bundles of money were beneath it, arranged so that they were only one layer deep. The bills were tied together with twine. Longarm picked up one of the bundles and riffled the edges of the bills. Twenties, all of them.

Unless he missed his guess, they were all counterfeit too, just like the bills that somebody had given Rodriguez to kill him. Rodriguez had died not knowing that he had put his life on the line for counterfeit money. The stuff was good, no doubt about that.

But then, it should have been good, considering it had been printed from the plates made by the master counterfeiter Edward Nowlan.

And here was a plentiful supply of the stuff, Longarm thought grimly, hidden in the bag of a United States senator. . . .

Chapter 11

Longarm put the counterfeit bills back in Padgett's valise and replaced the false bottom. Anyone checking on the money would assume that it had not been disturbed, which was exactly what Longarm wanted. He continued searching the other bags. He still hadn't found everything he was looking for.

Nor did he over the next half hour as he completed the search. The phony money was the only bit of evidence he had uncovered. It would be safe enough where it was, he reasoned. He came up on the toes of his flat-heeled boots and blew out the lantern, then made his way out of the darkened boxcar.

The moon had risen while he was conducting the search, he saw as he stepped back out onto the platform between cars. Silvery illumination washed down over the craggy landscape and glittered on the snowcaps of distant peaks. Longarm made his way through the cars, balancing himself against the slight swaying of the train with the ease of a veteran traveler. The lamps were turned low, and most people were asleep. He reached the private compartment where the Cassidy sisters were staying and rapped lightly on the door.

It opened immediately, and one of the lovely young women looked out at him with a worried frown on her face. From her outfit, which was a simple traveling gown devoid of lace and foofaraws, Longarm judged her to be Julie. Even after all this time, he occasionally had trouble telling them apart—when they were dressed, that is.

His guess as to the identity of the blonde facing him was confirmed when she said anxiously, "Oh, Custis, I'm glad you're here. Have you seen Janice?"

Longarm frowned back at her. "I figured the two of you would be here together."

Julie took hold of his sleeve and practically pulled him into the compartment. She was stronger than she looked. "Janice said she was going to step out for a breath of fresh air. That was over half an hour ago, and she hasn't come back. To tell the truth, I thought she might have gone looking for you, intending to have you to herself for a while. That was why I asked if you'd seen her."

Longarm shook his head and said, "Sorry, I sure haven't. But I reckon she's bound to be all right. Nothing's going to happen to her here on the train—"

He stopped abruptly, realizing that not everyone on board this train was really what they were pretending to be. His discovery tonight was proof of that. "Tell you what," he went on. "I'll take a look around, see if I can find Janice. Will you be all right here?"

Julie nodded. "Worried, but all right. Actually, I think I ought to come with you."

"Nope," Longarm said firmly. "I want at least one of you ladies where I know I can find you, where I know you'll be safe."

She clutched at his arm. "You don't think Janice is safe?"

"I didn't say that. We've got to eat the apple one bite at a time, and I reckon the first bite is to find your sister."

He stepped out of the compartment and closed the door softly behind him, taking with him the image of Julie standing there with her lower lip caught between her white teeth, the worried frown creasing the tanned skin of her forehead.

Longarm knew that Janice was not behind him on the train, since he had just come from that direction. There were several passenger cars between this one and the engine, including the one where Senator Padgett's compartment was located, so he decided to work toward the front. If he had to, he could always bring the conductor and the porters in on the search, but he wanted to avoid raising that much of a commotion if at all possible.

As it turned out, he didn't have to go far at all. He made his way through the next car without seeing any sign of Janice, walked through the car after that with the same lack of results, then opened the door onto the platform between cars and saw two shadowy figures standing there in the moonlight. He recognized the sort of feathered hat that Janice preferred perched on the head of one of the figures. Standing next to her was a short, slender man. Longarm opened his mouth and was about to say something when the man suddenly threw his arms around Janice and pulled her against him.

Longarm stiffened and reached for his gun, but the sound of a wet, sloppy kiss, followed by the sharp crack of a slap, made him pause. Maybe he wasn't interrupting anything except an ill-timed romantic overture.

"How dare you!" Janice said shrilly. "Unhand me this instant, Mr. Mercer!"

Longarm's eyes widened in surprise, but now that he came to think of it, the gent on the platform with Janice was undoubtedly built like Leon Mercer. A grin plucked at Longarm's mouth as he watched Janice put her hands against the man's narrow chest and shove him away.

"I swear, I don't know what you were thinking of, Mr. Mercer!" said Janice, her voice a mixture of irritation and exasperation.

"Neither do I, Leon," Longarm said dryly as he stepped forward onto the platform and pulled the door shut behind him. No point in sharing this little domestic drama with anybody in the car behind him who happened to be awake at this late hour. "And you, Miss Janice," he went on, "I didn't expect to catch you sparking on a train platform with a respectable gent like Leon here."

"Custis!" exclaimed Janice. "What are you doing—I mean, how did you—I wasn't *sparking* with anyone!"

"Reckon I was mistaken, then. Sure looked to me like you and Leon were pretty wrapped up in each other."

"Well, it wasn't my idea, I assure you!"

Mercer said quickly, "It was all my fault, Marshal. I . . . I'm afraid I behaved like a dreadful cad. I'm ashamed to admit it, but I . . . I forced myself on poor Miss Cassidy." His voice was miserable and embarrassed, but it took on a moonstruck tone as he looked at Janice and added, "She was just so lovely, standing there in the moonlight, and I couldn't help myself."

Janice sniffed. "I suppose all men have such animal urges, but I expected better of you, Mr. Mercer. You're a gentleman. You should be able to control those impulses!"

Her injured tone might have struck Longarm as a little more genuine if he hadn't remembered the way she had hauled his manhood out of his trousers and played a tune on it the very first day they met. The blushing-virgin act wasn't very convincing now. Still, if she didn't want Leon Mercer to kiss her, she had every right to stop him.

Mercer gulped uneasily in the face of Janice's anger. "You won't tell the senator about this, will you? Either of you?"

"Well . . . I suppose it wouldn't serve any purpose to humiliate you," Janice allowed grudgingly. "Just as long as I have your assurance that it will never happen again."

"Never!" Mercer said hastily. "I swear it!"

She gave him a little smile. "I suppose I should be flattered, in a way. Why, to provoke such a response from a man I've always considered a bit of a cold fish . . ."

"That's exactly what I am," Mercer said. "A cold fish. But you are a beautiful woman, Miss Cassidy. A very beautiful woman."

Janice lifted her chin. "Thank you. Now, you run on back to the senator, and we won't say anything more about this. It will be as if it had never happened."

"Thank you, Miss Cassidy. Thank you so much."

For a second, Longarm thought Mercer was going to ruin things by slobbering all over Janice in his gratitude, but then he backed off and disappeared into the next car, heading back to Padgett's compartment.

Janice chuckled and stepped over to Longarm, sliding her arm around his. "Can you believe that?" she asked. "I was just standing there talking to him, and suddenly that mousy little man had his arms around me, and—I swear it!—his tongue was halfway down my throat!"

"Leon got a mite carried away, all right," Longarm said. "But he was right about one thing—you do look beautiful in the moonlight. And in any *other* light I can think of."

Janice snuggled against him so that he could feel the warm, heavy weight of her breast on his arm. "Why, Custis, what a lovely thing to say. But I was just wondering . . . how did you happen to open that door at that very moment?"

"I was looking for you," Longarm told her. "Your sister's mighty worried about you."

"Julie sent you out looking for me?" Janice sounded surprised. "There was no need for that. I'm perfectly capable of taking care of myself!"

"Yes, ma'am, I'm sure you are. But I reckon sisters are supposed to worry. That's part of what makes 'em sisters."

"I suppose so. I just came out here for a breath of fresh air, you know . . . and then I ran into Mr. Mercer and we began talking. He surprised me. He's really a very charming man when he wants to be, quite funny and intelligent. But he's just so wrapped up in his work most of the time!"

"Leon's the dedicated type, all right," said Longarm. "You threw quite a scare into him tonight. I don't figure he'll ever bother you again." He urged Janice gently toward the door. "Now we'd better get back to your sister, so that you can put her mind at ease."

Longarm led her back to the compartment where Julie was waiting. When Julie opened the door and saw her sister standing there, she threw her arms around Janice and hugged her tightly. "I thought something terrible must have happened to you! Don't scare me that way again!"

"Oh, poo, it didn't amount to anything," Janice protested. "I simply had to fend off the amorous attentions of the senator's assistant, Mr. Mercer."

Julie leaned back and stared at Janice. "Mr. Mercer?" she repeated. "Are you sure?"

"He was kissing me passionately. I think I'm usually aware of who's doing something like that."

Julie laughed. "I might have expected such a thing from the senator himself . . . but Mr. Mercer?"

Longarm leaned against the compartment door, which he had closed behind him, and watched the two of them dissolve into a fit of giggles. After a moment he reminded them he was there by saying, "I sort of had in mind doing some passionate kissing of my own. . . ."

Julie turned and came into his arms. "Of course you did." She lifted her lips to his, and the kiss clung for a long moment that had his pulse racing faster than any thoroughbred. "Thank you for rescuing Janice from the clutches of Mr. Mercer."

"Wait just a minute," Janice protested. "Custis didn't have to rescue me. I handled the situation myself."

Longarm chuckled and told Julie, "She sure did. Had poor old Leon shaking in his spats."

Janice gently edged Julie aside and gave Longarm a kiss too. "But you were right there to help me in case I needed it," she whispered. "I appreciate that, Custis." Her hand dropped to his groin. "And I like to show my appreciation in tangible ways."

Over the next hour, both sisters showed their appreciation in ways so tangible that by the time they were through, Longarm felt as if he'd been turned inside out and drained of every bit of vitality. It was almost enough to distract him from the real reason he had gotten mixed up with these racing folks in the first place.

Almost . . .

•   •   •

After the night he'd spent, he had every right to feel groggy, but he woke up clearheaded and alert the next morning. He knew now what he had to do. This case was winding down at last, and he was more than ready for it to come to a successful conclusion.

The train reached Carson City around the middle of the day after that. Longarm had been to the capital city of Nevada many times, but he still enjoyed the clear, cool air and the majesty of the Sierra Nevada rising just to the east of town. The state capitol building with its white dome rising into the blue sky was an impressive structure as well, having been built some ten years earlier of native stone and massive wooden beams. Longarm could see the capitol from the train station. He could also see the racetrack on the eastern edge of town. As usual, it was the immediate destination of most of the people who disembarked from the train.

Longarm stuck with Senator Padgett and Leon Mercer, also as usual. Mercer hadn't been able to meet Longarm's eyes squarely ever since the night before last, but Padgett didn't seem to notice his assistant's embarrassment. Padgett wasn't the type to be too observant of the people who worked for him, Longarm thought. As long as they did their jobs and kept things running smoothly, that was all the senator cared about.

While the horses were getting settled in, Longarm wandered around the racetrack, familiarizing himself with the layout of the stands and the adjacent buildings. By the time Padgett was ready to head for the hotel, Longarm knew where everything was. He was satisfied that he would be able to find his way around in the dark.

The hotel was not far from the capitol, and Padgett had been able to book a suite of rooms. As Longarm walked into the sitting room, carrying his war bag and Winchester, he said, "I'll bunk out here on that big ol' sofa in the corner, Senator. You and Leon can each have a room to yourself."

"Why, thank you," said Padgett, the words sounding more sarcastic than sincere.

Longarm didn't care. Pretty soon, he wouldn't have to worry any more about riding herd on this arrogant politician.

The race was scheduled for the following afternoon. Longarm snatched a moment before it started to find the Cassidy sisters in the crowd. He gave each of them a hug and kiss, then said, "I've got a good feeling about this race, ladies. My hunch is that when it's over, you're going to have yourselves a winner."

"I hope so," Julie said fervently. "Matador's workouts yesterday afternoon and this morning were excellent. If he's ever going to do it, it might as well be now."

"Of course he's going to do it," Janice said. "You just wait and see!"

"I'll be pulling for him," Longarm promised. "Now I reckon I ought to get back to the senator."

He hesitated a moment longer, looking at the beautiful, anxious, hopeful faces of Janice and Julie Cassidy. If there was any justice in the world, he thought, Matador would come through for them today.

He made his way back to Padgett's box and found the senator fidgeting nervously with a cigar, waiting for the race to begin. "Where have you been?" Padgett snapped at Longarm.

"Just wishing Miss Julie and Miss Janice good luck today," said Longarm. He noticed how quickly Leon Mercer averted his eyes at the mention of Janice.

"Wishing them luck?" said Padgett. "Don't you think you ought to be hoping Caesar wins instead?"

Longarm took his seat in the box and suppressed the surge of irritation he felt. "Senator, I reckon you've forgotten . . . just because I'm following you around trying to make sure you stay alive, that doesn't mean I'm working for you. The Justice Department still pays my wages."

"Of course, of course," Padgett grumbled. "I just thought that since you're sitting in my box, you ought to root for my horse."

"Well, I wish you luck too, Senator. I wish everybody

in the race luck.'' Longarm held up his hands, palms out. ''Other than that, I'm impartial.''

''I suppose that's the best I can hope for.'' Padgett stuck the cigar in his mouth and clamped his teeth down on it. ''This is the worst part,'' he said around the cylinder of tobacco, ''waiting for the race to start.''

A few minutes later, the horses were brought to the starting line. The crowd filling the grandstands rose to its feet. The colors of the jockeys' silks were bright in the afternoon sun. Longarm had no trouble picking out the green shirt worn by Cy and the red shirt that Matador's rider sported. Both horses were toward the middle of the line. Not the most advantageous position, but not the worst either.

The stillness of anticipation, of hundreds of held breaths, fell over the track as the starter prepared to fire his pistol. When the sharp crack sounded, the horses surged forward in a mighty burst of muscle and sinew. A many-throated shout rose from the crowd.

Longarm had seen enough of these races by now to be aware of some of the patterns that developed. He saw the fast starter kick out to the front of the pack and build up a short lead that soon began to shrink as the horse faltered and the others in the race came on more strongly. He saw the horses that liked the turns and those that preferred the straightaways assert themselves in those places. The lead changed hands several times, and each time Longarm knew that that particular horse wouldn't be able to hold it. They each fell back in turn, and others took their places. Caesar and Matador continued to run just ahead of the middle of the pack. Both horses were strong finishers, Longarm knew, and they were both staying in position to make their move.

Once around the track, then twice, and now the horses were in the final circuit. As they approached the last turn, Padgett leaned forward, his face brick red, and bellowed, ''Now, Cy! Bring him on *now,* damn you!''

Cy couldn't have heard that shout over the thunderous pounding of hooves down there on the track, but as if Padgett's words had reached his ears, he began working the quirt harder on Caesar and drove the big blood bay forward at renewed speed. As the horses swept through the final turn, Caesar lunged toward the leaders, knifed among them, then darted ahead, wresting control of the lead for himself. Matador was still six horses back entering the home stretch.

Longarm bit back a groan. It looked as if Caesar was going to win again. He had honestly hoped—had felt certain—it was Matador's day at last.

That was when a streak of chestnut-brown lightning erupted down the track, passing horse after horse. Matador was coming on; his jockey had held one last spurt of speed in reserve. But would it be enough now, or had it come too late? Longarm found himself yelling, "Come on, Matador, come on!" as the chestnut drew closer and closer to the bay. He ignored the glower that Senator Padgett sent his way and kept cheering for Matador.

The finish line was close, maybe too close for Matador to catch up. His head was even with Caesar's rump. Caesar was losing something, though, Longarm saw suddenly. The big bay's gait wasn't quite as smooth as it had been a second earlier. Cy should have waited to make the move, Longarm realized. Caesar didn't have enough left to hold off Matador's charge.

Matador's head passed Caesar's shoulder, and then the two horses were running neck-and-neck as the finish line loomed right in front of them. With one final lunge, Matador extended himself, and although it was extremely close as the two horses flashed past the finish line, everyone in the stands knew who had won the race. It was Matador by a nose. Longarm whooped and thrust both clenched fists into the air.

Padgett cursed loudly, fluently, and profanely. He snatched off his soft felt hat, threw it on the floor of the box, and stomped on it in sheer rage and frustration and disappointment. Longarm turned to him, ignoring the way Mercer was desperately shaking his head in warning, and clapped a hand on the senator's shoulder. "Look at it this way, Senator," Longarm said, "at least your horse came in second."

"Second!" Padgett repeated in an injured tone at the top

of his lungs. "What damned good is second place? I *won* last time. From here on out, if I don't win I might as well come in last every time!"

Longarm just shook his head. He couldn't understand that reasoning. Second place wasn't bad—in anything except a gunfight.

"I'm going to congratulate the Cassidy sisters," he said to Padgett. "Don't you reckon you ought to come along?"

"I'm going to go fire Cy! He never should have made his move when he did. He should have waited and made Matador commit first."

Longarm didn't point out that Padgett had been yelling for Cy to bring Caesar on for several seconds before the jockey had actually done so. If Cy had not waited as long as he had, the race wouldn't have even been close.

Padgett sighed heavily and reached down to pick up his trampled hat. He tried to push it back into some semblance of its normal shape, finally gave up in disgust, and jammed the hat into his pocket. "All right!" he said. "I suppose I have to be a gentleman about this. Let's go down to the winner's circle."

Trailed by Mercer, Longarm and Padgett made their way through the crowd in front of the grandstand and reached the winner's circle after several minutes. Janice and Julie were there, tears of joy streaming down their faces as they hugged Matador, their jockey, their trainer, and each other. All the other owners were on hand to congratulate the Cassidy sisters, and their good wishes and excitement seemed genuine. Everyone was glad to see the lovely young blondes win for a change. They all knew how hard Janice and Julie had worked for this.

Padgett leaned over and kissed each of the sisters on the cheek. "Congratulations, my dears," he said over the hubbub surrounding them. "I'm glad Matador won." The words didn't sound like they choked him—too much.

Longarm threw his arms around Janice and Julie at the same time. "I told you it was Matador's day," he said. "And it's your day too."

"Thank you, Custis," Julie said somewhat breathlessly.

"I'm glad you're here to share this with us."

"So am I!" said Janice. She pulled Longarm's mouth down to hers, and whoops and cheers went up from the crowd as she kissed him.

Grinning, Longarm stepped back to let the twins bask in their glory a little while longer. He hated to think about ruining this celebration for them, but he still had a job to do, and for his purposes, this was the best place to wrap it up.

He slid his left hand into the pocket of his coat while his right hovered near the center of his body, not far from the walnut grips of his .44. His coat was pushed back a little, giving him easy access to the cross-draw rig. With his left hand, he took a bundle of the counterfeit money from his pocket. He had slipped into the senator's room earlier in the day while no one was around and removed it from the false bottom of Padgett's valise.

"Senator," he said loudly, "I think you lost something."

Padgett turned toward him, a puzzled frown on his beefy face, and Longarm tossed the bundle of bills at him. Instinctively, Padgett reached up to catch the money and exclaimed, "What—"

Longarm drew the Colt, leveled it, and cocked it in the same motion. The sight of the gun brought startled curses from several of the horse owners and the other bystanders, and quite a few of them began scrambling backward to get out of the way of any gunfire. "Don't move, Senator," Longarm said as the winner's circle practically cleared out around them. A few yards away, Janice and Julie Cassidy were staring at him in a mixture of confusion and horror, as was Leon Mercer.

Padgett recovered his tongue first. "What the bloody hell is this all about?" he demanded furiously. "Put that gun down, Marshal!"

Longarm shook his head slowly. "You're under arrest, Senator, for murder, conspiracy, and possession of counterfeit money."

"Counterfeit money? Possession? You threw it at me!"

Padgett shook the bundle of bills at Longarm, his hand trembling from the depth of his emotion.

"There's plenty more where that came from, hidden in the false bottom of one of your bags."

"That's a lie! I never saw this money before, or any other counterfeit money!" Padgett drew his shoulders back and puffed up his chest. "Have you forgotten who you're talking to, Marshal? By God, I'll have your badge for this! I'm going to wire Marshal Vail right now—"

Padgett started to take a step forward, but Longarm pointed the muzzle of the .44 right at his forehead, making him come to an abrupt stop. "I know who I'm talking to," Longarm said coolly. "I'm talking to a murdering bastard who used his position—a position the people of Colorado elected him to!—to organize a counterfeiting ring that could've brought the whole country's economy crashing down if you hadn't been stopped. Well, you *have* been stopped, here and now." Longarm waggled the barrel of his pistol. "I know you're carrying a gun, Senator. Take it out with your left hand, nice and easy, and put it on the ground."

Leon Mercer took a step toward Longarm, saying, "Marshal, this is insane! The senator couldn't have—"

"Back off, Leon, or I'll crack this six-shooter right across that bald noggin of yours!"

Mercer's eyes bugged out, and he stepped back with a frightened gulp.

Padgett regarded Longarm narrowly. "You're going to regret this, Long," he said. "You're going to regret this more than anything you've ever done in your life."

"I doubt it," Longarm said with a smirk. "What I really regret is voting for you a time or two before, back when I didn't know what a low-down skunk you really are."

Goaded beyond endurance, Padgett let out a howl and flung the bundle of phony bills back at Longarm. He charged right behind the money, swinging a fist at the lawman's head.

Longarm let the money bounce harmlessly off his chest and set his feet for the straight, hard punch he shot out with his left. His fist smashed into Padgett's mouth and snapped the senator's head back. Padgett flew backward, arms wind-milling, and crashed down heavily on his rump. Blood welled between his fingers as he pressed his hand to his pulped lips and groaned thickly.

Longarm stepped over to him, bent, and jerked the little pistol from the holster under Padgett's coat. "On your feet," he said grimly as he stepped back again. "I reckon, Senator, that your next term's going to be served behind bars."

Chapter 12

Well, thought Longarm as he was leaving the Carson City jail an hour or so later, that had gone about as well as could be expected. The sheriff and the jailer had been mighty impressed by the fact that they now had an actual United States senator locked up in their hoosegow. "Don't get used to it, boys," Longarm had warned them. "Most of them politicians are just too damned slick for us poor lawmen to ever catch up to 'em when they're up to no good."

The local badges had been disappointed when Longarm had said that he wanted to interrogate Padgett privately in the senator's cell. It was federal business, though, so they had reluctantly agreed and left Longarm alone with his prisoner in the cell block.

Now Longarm paused outside the jail and lit a cheroot, inhaling gratefully on the smoke. For the first time in quite a while, he didn't feel as if he had a bull's-eye painted on his back. He could go on about his business now without having to worry overmuch about anybody trying to kill him.

The first thing he wanted was some dinner. He headed for the hotel, and as he expected, quite a few people were waiting in the lobby to ask him questions. Most of them were horse owners or other folks connected with the racing circuit. They had witnessed his arrest of Miles Padgett and were burning up with curiosity.

Longarm held up his hands to quiet the crowd that formed around him. "I'm sorry, but I can't tell you folks anything. The arrest of Senator Padgett is strictly a federal matter, and I'm referring all questions to the Justice Department in Washington." He looked at a couple of reporters from the local newspaper, both of whom had their mouths open to shout questions at him. "That goes for you gentlemen of the press too," Longarm said. "If there's anything you want to know, you can wire Washington."

"But that's not fair, Marshal!" wailed one of the scribblers. "You're right here! Why can't you tell us all about it?"

"Because that's not my job," Longarm said. "My job's to bring in crooks who violate federal law, and that's what I've done. My part of it is finished."

Stubbornly, he ignored the other questions that were called out to him and pushed his way through the crowd. As he went up the stairs to the second floor, anxious to get back to the suite, he reflected that he hadn't seen the Cassidy sisters downstairs in the mob. He wondered where they were.

That question was answered a moment later when he unlocked his door and stepped into the sitting room. Janice and Julie were waiting for him there, Janice sitting in a wing-back armchair, Julie perched on the edge of the sofa. Both of them wore anxious expressions.

"We persuaded the desk clerk to let us wait in here for you," Julie explained quickly before Longarm could say anything. "I hope that's all right, Custis."

Longarm took off his hat and tossed it on the sofa. "Sure. What fella wouldn't like to come back to his hotel room and find a pair of beautiful ladies like you waiting for him?"

They ignored the compliment. Janice said, "Is it true? Have you really taken Senator Padgett off to jail?"

"That's where he belongs," Longarm said harshly. "Because of him, some good men are dead back in Albuquerque."

Julie shook her head. "I don't understand. I thought someone tried to kill the senator while we were in Albuquerque. At least that's what Mr. Mercer told us a little while ago. The poor man's so upset. I've never seen him so broken up. He refuses to believe that Senator Padgett could be guilty of anything."

"Well, it's good for a fella to believe in the man he works for."

So Mercer had spilled the story of the assassination attempt to the Cassidy sisters. Longarm wasn't particularly surprised. There was no point in keeping it a secret any longer.

"Is it true?" asked Janice. "Did someone try to kill Senator Padgett? Is that why you've been traveling with him ever since?"

Longarm sat down in the room's other armchair and stretched his legs out in front of him, crossing them at the ankle. He wished he had a glass of good Maryland rye. Explaining was usually thirsty work.

"I've been traveling with the senator and the rest of you racing folks because I figured somebody amongst you was a killer."

"You thought one of the other owners hired somebody to take a shot at the senator?" Julie exclaimed.

"Nope," Longarm said patiently. "I knew none of you were responsible for that shooting at the racetrack in Albuquerque. *I* was."

They both stared at him wide-eyed, utterly confused.

"It all goes back to a fella named Edward Nowlan," continued Longarm. "He was a counterfeiter, maybe the best engraver of phony printing plates to ever come down the pike. Me and some other marshals caught up to him in Albuquerque and busted up his operation. Nowlan got himself killed in the shooting. But he wasn't the boss of the whole thing; as good as he was at what he did, he was just another hired hand when you got right down to it. Somebody else organized all of it.''

''And you're accusing Senator Padgett of being this mysterious ringleader?'' asked Janice.

Longarm nodded and said, ''When I saw that Nowlan had a ticket for a horse race in his pocket when he died, I wondered if there was a connection. Nowlan was known to be all business, didn't care about anything except his engraving. It stood to reason that a fella like that wouldn't be going to a horse race for fun. But he might have been planning to go to meet his boss.''

''The senator,'' said Julie.

''I'm getting to that,'' Longarm said. ''When I went out to the race, I didn't even know Padgett would be there, let alone that he was part of the circuit now. But the more I thought about it, the more I realized what a good cover it would be for the ringleader to travel around from race to race. He could drop off some of the phony money at every stop for his agents to pass. Except he didn't have the money, because we confiscated it from the warehouse in Albuquerque where it was being stockpiled. We got the printing plates too, but we didn't manage to keep 'em because the other marshals were murdered and the plates stolen while I was at the race that first day.''

Janice shuddered. ''You mean someone killed those men just to get some . . . some printing plates?''

''Those plates are worth a fortune to the right folks,'' Longarm pointed out. ''The boss could always rebuild the operation, as long as he had the plates.''

Julie took a deep breath and said, ''All right, let me get this straight. You thought the ringleader of the counterfeiters was connected with the racing circuit and that he had stolen the plates back from your friends?''

''It was a hunch,'' Longarm admitted, ''but one that seemed to stand a good chance of being true. It was worth investigating, anyway. That was why I wired my boss and had him set up the phony assassination attempt on the senator.''

"The gunman wasn't really trying to kill Senator Padgett?" Janice asked.

"Nope, we just made it look good. Then, when I was assigned to protect him from any more assassination attempts, it gave me a perfect excuse to tag along with you folks and made it look too like the whole counterfeiting angle had been put aside for the time being. I didn't know then that Padgett had anything to do with Nowlan and the plates."

"So you were really after the leader of the counterfeiting ring, not some mysterious assassin?" Understanding was beginning to dawn on Julie's face.

"And I knew I was on the right track too when somebody tried to kill me that first night."

"What?" said Janice. "That's the first I've heard of an attempt on your life."

Longarm nodded soberly. "Somebody clouted me over the head with a two-by-four and tried to push me off the train while it was passing over the Rio Grande between Albuquerque and El Paso." He saw Julie blush slightly, and knew she was remembering what else had happened on that train platform that night. "When I got back to the senator's compartment," Longarm went on, "he was unaccounted for. That was the first inkling I had that he might be involved with the case. If he was the ringleader, he sure wouldn't want me tagging along. He'd be afraid I might stumble over some evidence linking him with the counterfeiters—which is exactly what finally happened. That pile of phony money hidden in his valise is proof he was involved up to his neck."

"It's amazing," Janice said, "the way you were able to piece all this together, Custis."

Longarm shrugged modestly. "I've tracked down more than a few no-good scalawags. They always slip up somewhere and give themselves away."

Julie said, "It certainly sounds like you have a solid case against the senator. I guess we'll have to believe what you've told us about him, whether we really want to or not." She smiled sadly. "He was a bit crude sometimes, but I hate to think he was actually a cold-blooded killer.''

"Oh, he never got his own hands dirty, but he sure paid for those killings. He had me bushwhacked in Tucson too, and it's no fault of his that I'm still here drawing breath.''

"What about the printing plates?" Janice asked. "Have you found them yet?"

Longarm's jaw clenched. "Not yet. I spent an hour talking to Padgett after I locked him up, and he never said one word about where they were hidden. I reckon they'll turn up sooner or later, though. The important thing now is that Padgett's behind bars where he belongs.'' The big lawman leaned forward and pushed himself to his feet. "And I'm mighty hungry. Will you two ladies join me for supper?"

"The dining room is liable to be a madhouse," warned Julie.

Longarm reached for his hat. "Maybe so, but my stomach thinks my throat's been cut. I need to get on the outside of a surrounding.''

Both young women laughed. "Of course we'll go with you, Custis,'' Janice said. "We'd never turn down your company.''

As he went out arm in arm with them, Longarm said, "I'm mighty sorry about ruining your little celebration in the winner's circle this afternoon. I wanted to take Padgett by surprise, so that he wouldn't put up much of a fight. That seemed to be a good time and place.''

"You took him by surprise, all right. You took all of us by surprise.''

"At least Matador won. Another couple of days like this, and you two can afford to do just about anything you want with that ranch of yours.''

"That's right," Janice said with a smile. "If this keeps up, we're going to be rich. . . .''

The hotel dining room was indeed crowded, and Longarm was the recipient of at least a hundred curious stares. He ignored all of them and concentrated on enjoying his dinner with the Cassidy sisters.

They were having coffee after the meal when Janice

looked up and suddenly gasped in alarm, "Custis!"

Longarm saw that she was gazing past his shoulder, and twisted his head so that he could see what was coming at him. Leon Mercer was stalking through the dining room with the awkward, determined, overly cautious gait of a man unaccustomed to drinking who has just put away a considerable amount of whiskey. His coat was rumpled, his tie was askew, and he wasn't wearing a hat. Several strands of the dark hair that was normally combed across his balding head stood up in the air at odd angles. Mercer blinked rapidly as his bleary eyes tried to focus on Longarm. He said in a loud, angry voice, "Ah, ha! So there you are, you traitor!"

Carefully, Longarm placed his napkin beside his plate and stood up, turning as he did so to face Mercer. "Hello, Leon," he said. "What can I do for you?"

"You can march right over to the jail and release the finest politician who ever drew breath!" Mercer said thickly. "You had no right to lock up Senator Padgett!"

The dining room had fallen silent, and every eye in the place was fixed on this confrontation. Longarm said, "The senator broke the law, Leon. I didn't have any choice but to arrest him."

"That's insane! It's not . . . not possible! Miles Padgett is an honorable man—"

"I'm not going to stand here and argue with you," Longarm cut in. "What's done is done." His tone was gentler as he went on. "Looks to me like you've had a few too many jolts of Who-Hit-John, Leon. Maybe you'd better go back up to your room and try to get some sleep. That'd be the best thing in the world for you."

"Sleep?" Mercer repeated in a high-pitched, incensed voice. "Sleep? How can I sleep when an innocent man has been thrown behind bars by a brutal minion of the law? What have you done to him? If you've hurt the senator, I . . . I'll kill you!"

With that, he reached under his coat and jerked out a small pocket pistol.

Longarm grimaced. The gun in Mercer's hand wasn't

161

much more than a toy, but somebody could still get hurt if he started waving it around and it went off. One long, quick stride brought Longarm close to Mercer, and his fingers closed around the wrist of the smaller man. His other hand caught hold of the pistol's cylinder so that it couldn't turn. A sharp twist was all it took. Mercer yelped and let go of the gun.

Longarm stuck the pistol in his coat pocket. Mercer put his hands over his face and began to sob. "Come on now, Leon," Longarm said as he put an arm around Mercer's shoulders. "I ain't going to hold this against you, because I know how upset you are. Here, let me help you upstairs."

Mercer pulled away from him with a burst of unexpected strength. "No! Stay away from me! I won't let you arrest me too!"

"I got no reason to arrest you, Leon. I don't reckon you knew a thing about what Padgett was up to. He fooled you just like he fooled everybody else."

That seemed to make Mercer feel even worse. He dropped into an empty chair and started crying harder. Longarm looked around for help.

Janice stood up and came over to him. "Perhaps I can talk to him," she said. In a whisper, she added, "We both know Mr. Mercer is rather fond of me."

Longarm recalled how Mercer had grabbed Janice on the train and kissed her. Mercer wasn't in any shape now for such shenanigans. "All right," he said. "Maybe you can talk some sense into him."

While Longarm and Julie watched, Janice talked to Mercer in a low-pitched voice, and after a few minutes, she looked up at Longarm to say, "I'll see that he gets back to his room. I think he'll be all right."

"Are you sure that's a good idea, Janice?" asked Julie.

Janice continued patting Mercer on the back as she rolled her eyes at her sister. "I'll be fine," she said. She took hold of Mercer's arm and helped him to his feet, and then the two of them made their way out of the dining room.

"Janice has a good heart," Julie said. "She'll straighten out Mr. Mercer."

162

"Maybe so," said Longarm as he sat down again.

Julie reached across the table and rested her hand on his. "I suppose you'll be leaving the racing circuit now."

"No reason for me to keep traveling with it," he said.

"Then we'll have to make your farewell *special*. We haven't really finished celebrating Matador's victory, you know."

Longarm had to grin. He was all for celebrating.

Unfortunately, there wasn't enough time for a proper celebration tonight. When they reached the Cassidy sisters' room, Longarm had to content himself with a long, hot kiss from Julie, who wrapped her arms around his neck and clung tightly to him. Her breasts flattened against his chest and he felt himself responding, especially when her tongue slipped into his mouth and began exploring wetly. Not wanting either of them to get too worked up to stop, Longarm gently disengaged himself from her embrace.

"What's wrong?" Julie asked with a frown. "I thought we were going to have a good time."

"Well, Janice isn't here," Longarm said.

"She won't mind if we start without her," Julie said with a wicked smile.

The prospect was appealing to Longarm. Although sharing a bed with both of the twins at the same time had been mighty pleasurable, there was a part of him that still found it odd and a mite uncomfortable. Deep down, he preferred the arrangement of one man and one woman, doing their damnedest to love each other to death. He was just an old stick-in-the-mud, he told himself.

But more importantly, he had other things to do tonight. This case wasn't finished yet, but it was sure closing in. Before the night was over, he hoped to discover everything else he needed to know.

"I've got to run an errand, Julie," he said, trying not to wince at the mixture of anger and disappointment that appeared on her face.

"What sort of errand?" she demanded.

"Law business," he answered vaguely.

163

"And it won't wait?"

"Afraid not."

"Well, will it take very long?"

"Don't know," Longarm replied honestly. "Might not. Then again, it could take most of the night."

"Most of the night!" she practically yelped. "Custis, I . . . I don't believe this."

Longarm stepped over to her and brushed his lips across her forehead. "Then believe how sorry I am," he said, and he meant every word of it—in more ways than one.

He slipped out of the room before Julie could protest anymore, but he carried the image of her face with him. It haunted him as he left the hotel and headed on foot for the racetrack.

Carson City, despite being the capital of Nevada, was a small town. The walk out to the racetrack was a fairly easy one on this cool, clear, high country evening.

The place was dark when Longarm got there, just as he had expected. He made his way directly to the stables. There was a watchman on duty, but he was an old man, probably had been a cowhand until the years had crippled him too much for that job, and he was dozing on a chair leaned back against the wall of the paddock. Longarm left him there sleeping and moved on into the wide aisle between the stalls.

Several of the horses whinnied when they caught his scent. Longarm said, "Shhh," and softly sang a fragment of one of the many songs he had learned back in his cowboying days. The melodies were meant to soothe a restless herd of cattle on a long, lonesome trail, but they worked pretty well with horses too. Some of the thoroughbreds still stamped and snuffled in their stalls, but for the most part they quieted down.

Enough moonlight and starlight came in through the big, open doors of the building for Longarm to see fairly well as he made his way along the aisle toward the smaller door at the far end. That door, he knew, led into the jockeys' dressing room and the storage room. All the riders' gear was still there, even though the race was over, because the horses would be put through another workout in the morning before boarding the train for the run up to Reno. Longarm reached the door and tried the knob.

Locked.

He grimaced. That would slow him down a little, but it wouldn't stop him. He took a ring of keys from his coat pocket and began trying them. The fourth one he slipped into the lock worked well enough to turn the tumblers, though it grated a bit as he did so. With a little pressure judiciously applied to the knob, it turned and the door opened.

Longarm eased it shut behind him after gliding into the storage room. He found himself in utter blackness, because this chamber underneath the grandstands was windowless. His fingers delved into his pocket and found a match. He scratched the lucifer into life, squinting his eyes against its sulfurous glare. Moving quickly before the match burned out, he located a lantern and lit it. A yellow, flickering glow filled the room as he lowered the lantern's chimney.

The light showed him exactly what he expected to find: saddles perched on sawhorses, harnesses and bridles hanging from hooks on the walls, saddle blankets, extra stirrups, trunks full of assorted gear.

All of these things had traveled on the train in the cars where the horses had ridden. They had not been carried in the normal baggage car. Longarm had searched the regular baggage and found nothing except the counterfeit money hidden in Senator Padgett's valise. If those printing plates were still anywhere in the vicinity, they had to be here somewhere. Of course, the ringleader could have passed them on to a confederate by now, but Longarm doubted that had happened. For one thing, knowing how valuable those plates were, the boss would not have wanted to let them very far out of his sight. He would want them somewhere close by, so that he could check on them often and make sure they were still all right.

Longarm started looking. He concentrated on the trunks full of equipment, since there were no hiding places on the stripped-down racing saddles. His frustration grew as a quarter of an hour, then a half hour, passed with him finding no sign of the plates. Surely his theory had not been wrong. The phony bills hidden in Padgett's valise proved that the ringleader was part of the racing circuit. Longarm had eliminated all the other hiding places.

There were several personal bags belonging to the jockeys. Longarm started in on them next. He paid particular attention to Cy's bag. Though he had written off the young man as a possible member of the gang, something could have been hidden in Cy's gear without the jockey being aware of it. But there was nothing unusual to be found there, and Longarm had to bite back a curse as he tossed Cy's bag onto the floor near Caesar's saddle. Maybe his reasoning had been wrong, Longarm told himself. He had thought that his line of logic ran true from point to point, but maybe he had missed a turn. It had happened before, rarely to be sure—but it *had* happened.

The next bag belonged to Matador's rider. Longarm opened it, took out a set of silks, and placed them to the side. He found a quirt in the bag as well, and in the bottom of it a set of cloth-covered weights such as all the jockeys carried. With a sigh, he started to put the heavy, rectangular weights back in the bag.

Then he froze abruptly. He hefted the weights in his left hand, a frown appearing on his face. With his right hand, he reached into his trousers pocket and found his clasp knife. He brought it out, opened the blade, and with utmost caution pressed the sharp tip through the thick cloth. He cut a long slit with the knife, then put it away. Turning the weights over, he pulled the slit open.

The counterfeit printing plates slid out of the cloth cover into his hand.

After a moment, Longarm realized he wasn't breathing as he stared down at the pieces of gray, ink-stained metal. Three good men, three fellow marshals, had died violent deaths back in Albuquerque for these plates. There was no way of knowing how many phony bills were floating around that had been manufactured by Edward Nowlan using these plates. As Longarm had told Julie Cassidy, in the right hands they were worth a fortune.

And thinking about Julie reminded Longarm just where he had found them.

"Son of a bitch," said Longarm, quietly but fervently. He had been hoping he was wrong about his suspicions, but it looked like his hunch had been correct. One or both of the Cassidy sisters was mixed up in this, all the way to their pretty necks. He recalled that they needed money to get their horse ranch in Missouri back on its feet.

What better way to get money than to print your own?

He had been listening with one ear for the horses in the stalls outside, knowing that if anyone entered the stable they would probably make some noise and alert him. So far, they had been quiet. So it came as a surprise when one of the floorboards suddenly creaked behind him. His left hand tightened on the printing plates and his right darted toward the gun holstered on his hip as he started to turn.

A cold ring of metal—unmistakably the barrel of a gun—was jabbed hard against his neck, and a man's voice said in low and deadly tones, "Don't move, Marshal."

Chapter 13

"Howdy, Leon," Longarm said, forcing his voice to remain calm and steady. "Be careful with that pistol, old son. We don't want it to go off."

"That's right," said another voice. "We don't want blood all over the floor in here. The horses might smell it, and you know how spooky the scent of blood can make them."

Longarm closed his eyes for a second. There was a cold, hard ball of something—disgust, maybe—in his belly. All he had to go by were a few minor differences in tone and inflection, but he felt pretty confident he was right as he said, "Hello, Janice. I was truly hoping I was wrong about you."

She laughed. "What do you mean, wrong about me? You didn't have a clue what was really going on. My God, you arrested Senator Padgett! He's probably the only man in the world dumber than you."

"All right, that's enough," snapped Leon Mercer. "What are we going to do about this?"

"You know what we have to do," Janice said. "We have to kill him. But I want it to look like an accident."

Longarm heard another pistol being cocked. "I'll cover him. You drag that old man in here."

The gun went away from Longarm's neck. Mercer reached around him and plucked the .44 from the cross-draw rig. "Just so you don't get any ideas," Mercer said.

"Oh, I've got some ideas, all right," said Longarm. "Just wish a few of 'em had occurred to me earlier."

They didn't know about the derringer in his vest pocket. That might give him an advantage later on, but whether or not it would be enough to save his bacon, he didn't know.

He heard Mercer's footsteps retreating, and he said to Janice, "Mind if I turn around? I sort of like to see whoever's pointing a gun at me."

"All right. But be careful. I honestly don't want to shoot you, Custis."

Longarm kept his hands where she could see them as he turned to face her. She looked as lovely as ever in the lantern light, but those blue eyes had lost any warmth they had once possessed. Now they were like chips of ice.

"You couldn't stop interfering, could you?" she said, and he thought he heard a trace of genuine regret in her voice. "You had to keep poking around until we have no choice but to get rid of you."

Longarm hefted the printing plates, which he still held in his left hand. "These are worth a lot to you, aren't they?"

"They're worth the world," Janice said fervently. "They represent not having to struggle anymore. I can get away from that horrible horse ranch at last."

"Julie feel the same way?"

Janice laughed humorlessly. "Julie actually *likes* horses. She doesn't know anything about my . . . arrangement . . . with Leon."

"Did he recruit you to help him out in Albuquerque, or have you been part of the counterfeiting ring all along?"

"Leon organized the operation," Janice admitted. "He financed Nowlan with funds that he diverted from the senator's campaigns. But we met back East, while I was in school, and we each knew immediately that we'd encoun-

170

tered a kindred spirit. Leon influenced the senator to buy Caesar so that we could use the racing circuit as a cover for distributing the money.''

Longarm knew the only reason she was telling him all this was because she didn't expect him to be alive much longer. That was confirmed a moment later when Mercer dragged the body of the elderly watchman into the stable. The man's hat had fallen off, and Longarm could see the swollen lump on his head where somebody had clouted him. Longarm hoped the old man was just unconscious and not already dead—although if Mercer and Janice had their way, it wouldn't really matter.

''I was thinking that there might be a fire here in the stables,'' Mercer said as he straightened from his task. ''A regrettable thing, of course, but at least some of the horses will survive. Too bad that Marshal Long and the watchman here will both die in their valiant effort to free the horses.''

Janice nodded. ''I like it. That way any evidence will be destroyed in the fire.''

''Exactly.''

It could work, Longarm realized. Folks would be bound to wonder what he had been doing out here at the racetrack when disaster struck, but it would go down as an unanswered question. There would be nothing linking Janice and Mercer to his death.

''I want Caesar left in here to burn with Long and the old man,'' Mercer said. He laughed harshly. ''Not only is Padgett locked up for something he had nothing to do with, but he's going to lose that precious racehorse of his too.''

Janice shrugged. ''Some of the horses won't make it out of the fire. It'll look more realistic that way. I don't care if Caesar is one of them. I want Matador out, though.''

''I thought you didn't like horses,'' commented Longarm.

Janice looked squarely at him. ''I won't hurt Julie if I don't have to.''

''But if she got in your way, then she'd have to die too, right?''

Janice lifted the pistol in her hand. ''That's enough out

of you, Custis. You don't have any idea what my life has been like. You never even suspected either of us.''

''Well, that ain't strictly true,'' Longarm said, hoping that he could keep them talking and postpone his fate for a while. ''I knew almost from the start that Leon might be mixed up in the whole mess.''

Mercer gave a bark of laughter. ''Don't be ridiculous! You never suspected me.''

''As a matter of fact, I did. When I got back to the senator's compartment that night after we left Albuquerque and found out he could've been the one who tried to toss me off in the Rio Grande, I knew that *you* were just as much of a suspect as he was, Leon. You couldn't account for Padgett's whereabouts—but *he* couldn't account for *yours* either. And then you were the one who saw me poking around the jockeys' room in El Paso, and that had to spook you. As soon as we got to Tucson, you started scouting around for a way to get rid of me. The senator played right into your hands by starting that fracas with those two proddy *bandidos,* Rodriguez and Guzman. You paid 'em off with some of that counterfeit money to bushwhack me; only Rodriguez got himself killed and Guzman must've decided he didn't want to try me after all. You figured then that since I wasn't going away, you might as well try to throw me off the track, so you planted those phony bills in the senator's bag, hoping I'd find 'em and blame the whole thing on Padgett.''

''And that's exactly what happened,'' Mercer said proudly. ''You arrested him, and it never even occurred to you that his mousy little assistant might be the real brains. Hell, I've been pulling his strings all these years in the Senate, and no one ever gives me any credit for that either!''

''Mighty sorry to bust up your little play-pretty, Leon, but that arrest was as phony as those twenty-dollar bills Nowlan was printing up for you. Oh, the senator didn't know what I was doing when I braced him after the race this afternoon, but I explained it all to him in the jail later.

172

Apologized for having to punch him too. But you got to admit it made the whole thing look real.''

"You're lying," Mercer said with a sneer. "I fooled you, just like I fooled everybody else. You might as well admit it.''

Longarm shrugged. "Nope. I was just trying to make you think you were safe, Leon. I wanted to find those plates, and I figured you might let down your guard with the senator behind bars. Didn't figure on you following me out here.''

"We didn't," Janice said. "We were on our way to get the plates, and we just happened to see you slipping in here ahead of us." She shook her head regretfully. "I was really hoping you wouldn't find them, Custis. I hoped you weren't even looking for them anymore. But that's what it's all been about, hasn't it, right from the start? That's why you staged that assassination attempt in Albuquerque.''

"Janice told me about that," said Mercer. "I'll give you a little credit, Long, that was pretty tricky. I thought some lunatic was really after the senator at first. It gave you the perfect excuse to worm your way into my affairs.''

"But you still figured it'd be better if I wasn't around, so you jumped me on that train platform and tried to shove me off," Longarm said.

Mercer smiled. "It never hurts to simplify things whenever possible." The smile disappeared, and he gestured sharply with the gun in his hand. "There's been enough talking. More than enough. Turn around, Long.''

"Going to knock me out and tie me up 'fore you start that fire?" guessed Longarm.

"That's right. The ropes will burn up in the blaze, and no one will be able to tell you were tied. We'll put both of you near the entrance, so it'll look like you were trying to escape when the smoke and the flames overwhelmed you.''

Longarm took a deep breath. The derringer held two shots, so he would have a chance to down both of them. Not a *good* chance, mind you, but at least a chance. "Mind if I have a last cheroot?" His hand drifted toward his vest, as if he was reaching for a cigar.

Then Mercer yelled, ''No!'' as Longarm's hand dipped suddenly toward the pocket where the derringer was hidden. He slashed at Longarm with the gun in his hand. Longarm twisted aside from the blow and drove his left elbow into Mercer's side. Mercer gasped in pain and staggered to the side as Longarm palmed out the derringer.

Janice fired her gun at that moment, and what felt like a giant hand slapped the side of Longarm's head. He toppled to the hard-packed dirt floor of the stable, the derringer slipping out of his fingers as he fell. Waves of darkness rolled toward him.

''Hurry!'' he heard Janice saying, as if from a great distance. ''That shot may draw attention! We have to hurry!''

He felt hands grab him and start to drag him, but then the darkness caught up to him and washed over him, wiping out everything else.

He woke to a loud crackling and the frantic whinnying of terrified horses. Thick, acrid smoke stung his nose and eyes. Blinking rapidly against the tears that filled his eyes, he rolled onto his back and kicked his way into a sitting position. He had already figured out that his hands were tied together behind his back.

Longarm's head hurt like the very blazes, but his thinking was clear enough. Janice's bullet must have creased him, he thought, clipping his head just enough to knock him senseless for a few minutes. He could sense that he had not been unconscious for long. Long enough, though, for the two of them to tie him up and start the fire that was even now consuming the stable around him.

He was sitting with his back toward the building's entrance, he realized. As he started trying to turn around, someone suddenly grabbed his hands. A woman's voice shouted over the roar of the fire and the screams of the horses, ''Be still, Custis! I'll have you loose in a minute!''

Longarm twisted his head and saw her kneeling behind him, and thought for a second that Janice had relented and come back to free him. Then, as a knife began to saw at the ropes around his wrists, he realized that it was Julie rescuing him, not Janice.

"What are you doing here?" he bellowed.

"I followed you!" Sobs wracked her even as she worked at his bonds, and he suspected not all of them were caused by the smoke. "I wanted to see what you were doing that was so mysterious! I . . . I almost wish I hadn't found out!"

Longarm knew what she meant. She must have over-heard the conversation he'd had with Janice and Mercer. Julie had to know now that her sister was part of Mercer's murderous schemes.

The ropes parted under the knife in Julie's hand. She had only nicked Longarm a couple of times while she was cut-ting him loose. As he pushed himself a little unsteadily to his feet, she caught hold of his arm and gestured toward his head with her other hand. "You're hurt!"

Longarm knew she was pointing at the gash on his nog-gin where Janice's shot had grazed him. "It'll be all right!" he assured her. "Now, you'd better get out of here while you still can!" He began looking around for the uncon-scious watchman.

The man had regained consciousness, but he was trussed up the way Longarm had been, and there was a gag in his mouth as well. His rheumy eyes were wide and bulging with fear. Longarm took the knife from Julie, bent over the watchman, and began cutting the ropes. Over his shoulder, he said again to Julie, "Get out of here!"

"I'm going to let the other horses loose!" she cried, ignoring his command.

Longarm bit back a curse as Julie darted away along the center aisle of the stable. Several empty stalls full of hay were blazing intensely, and flames were beginning to climb up the walls of the stable. If the fire continued to spread, not only would this building be engulfed, but the adjacent grandstands would probably go up in flames too. There was nothing he could do about that; the conflagration was al-ready too far advanced. All he could hope for was to get himself and Julie and the old man out of there.

The ropes fell away from the watchman's wrists as Longarm finished cutting them. He tossed the knife aside and grabbed the old man's arms, lifting him to his feet. "Move, old-timer!" Longarm shouted at him, pushing him toward the entrance.

By this time, Julie had opened a couple of the stalls that were still occupied. A glance around the stable told Longarm about half of the racehorses were gone, freed no doubt by Mercer and Janice as they started the blaze. The two horses Julie had just freed galloped wildly out of their stalls, forcing her to jump back out of their way. As the animals disappeared into the thickening smoke, Longarm hoped they wouldn't get confused and run right back into the burning stable once they reached the outside. Horses had been known to do that very thing.

Longarm saw the watchman stumbling toward the entrance; then he turned toward the other stalls. He knew Julie wouldn't leave until all the horses were rescued, so the quickest way for both of them to get out would be for him to help her. He flung open the gate on one of the occupied stalls, and the desperate horse inside lunged past him, heading for the entrance.

New voices made his head jerk around. He heard Janice Cassidy say, "I tell you, I think I saw Julie come running in here!"

"Damn it, Janice, come back here!" shouted Leon Mercer.

The smoke billowing through the stable parted at that instant, and by the hellish light of the flames, Longarm clearly saw Janice and Mercer near the entrance. Janice was trying to come farther into the stable, but Mercer had hold of her arm and was tugging her away. Suddenly, the terrified horse Longarm had just freed loomed up in front of them, racing away from the smoke and flames. Mercer yelped in panic, released Janice's arm, and threw himself to the side, out of the way of the galloping beast.

Janice was not that fast—or that lucky.

Longarm winced as he saw and heard the horse run into Janice. She was knocked off her feet, and the horse's iron-shod hooves thudded into her as he trampled her. Longarm looked away as one of the hooves struck Janice in the face, destroying forever the beauty that had been hers.

"*Janice!*" The horrified scream came from Julie.

The flames had reached the roof now. There was no time for anything except getting out of there. Longarm lunged toward Julie, grabbed her arm, and pulled her toward the entrance. She tried to jerk away from him as they passed Janice's body, so he scooped her completely off the ground and tossed her over his shoulder. Lowering his throbbing head, he ran toward the open doors, following the clouds of smoke as they sought the night air. He had lost track of the watchman, and could only hope the old man had made it out safely. Mercer was gone too, having scurried away into the darkness as the horse was trampling Janice.

Behind Longarm, blazing beams began to plummet from the burning roof of the stable. . . .

Fresh air had never tasted so good. Longarm drew great breaths of it as he stumbled to safety, carrying a coughing, struggling Julie Cassidy. He was coughing quite a bit himself. The heat and smoke had seared his nose, throat, and lungs. A pounding like the drumming of a mad Indian filled his head. But now that he and Julie were safe, one thought clamored wildly for his attention.

Leon Mercer was still out there somewhere.

Mercer had to have the printing plates. He was probably heading for the hotel, Longarm thought. He didn't know if Mercer had seen him there in the stable or not. It was possible Mercer still thought he was tied up, perishing in the fire. In that case, Mercer would most likely return to the hotel and try to pick up the threads of his life. He had lost his partner, but he had the plates, and that was all Mercer really cared about, Longarm realized.

The man was in for one hell of a surprise.

A big, bulky shape appeared out of the darkness as Longarm set Julie on her feet again. She tried to run toward the stable, but Longarm caught her shoulders and held her back. At that moment, the roof collapsed, sending flames and sparks shooting high into the sky. Nothing in there could have survived the inferno. The grandstands were on fire now too, just as Longarm had feared.

Shouts of alarm made him look around, and he saw a large crowd running toward the fire from Carson City. Something nudged Julie, and Longarm felt it as well. Matador was there, bumping her shoulder with his nose, obviously seeking to make sure she was all right. The horse was what he had seen coming up to them out of the shadows a moment earlier, Longarm realized.

He saw one of the local lawmen, and grabbed the man's arm. "Hang on to Miss Cassidy here!" he ordered. "Don't let her go back in there!"

The man cast a dubious glance toward the burning stable. "Why would anybody *want* to?" he asked.

"Her sister's in there," Longarm said in a low, grim voice.

The man nodded, and he put an arm around the sobbing Julie, patting her awkwardly on the back. Longarm hoped he could trust the local badge to keep Julie out of trouble.

He had something else he had to do.

Grabbing Matador's mane, he swung up onto the thoroughbred's bare back. Matador danced around skittishly, unaccustomed to being ridden without a saddle, as well as to the much greater weight of Longarm, who would make two of some of the jockeys. "Come on, Matador!" Longarm called as he drove the heels of his boots into the chestnut's flanks.

Matador lunged forward into a gallop. Longarm controlled the horse with his knees and the hold he had on Matador's mane. The thoroughbred ran gamely through the night, pounding through the outskirts of Carson City before reaching the main street. Longarm swung Matador into the street and rode toward the hotel. The broad avenue was practically deserted at the moment, since nearly everyone in town was out at the racetrack watching the fire.

Longarm spotted one figure further along the street, however. A short, slender man who was hurrying toward the hotel as fast as he could without drawing attention to himself by actually running. At the sound of Matador's hooves, the man looked back, and he stopped in his tracks for a second as he saw the big U.S. marshal galloping straight toward him.

Leon Mercer let out a harsh, strangled cry of surprise and fear.

Longarm swept down the street toward him like an angel on horseback, an avenging angel come to exact retribution for all the deaths Mercer had caused. Mercer jerked his gun from under his coat and brought the weapon up in a trembling hand. He began to fire, jerking off shot after shot.

Longarm heard a couple of the slugs whine past his head. Those were the only ones that came close enough for him to hear. He rode into the face of Mercer's gunfire. The hammer of Mercer's gun clicked on an empty chamber. With another inarticulate cry, Mercer flung the now-useless weapon toward the onrushing Longarm and turned to run.

Veering Matador to the side, Longarm left the thoroughbred's back in a long, flat dive that sent him smashing into Mercer, his shoulder catching the fleeing man in the small of the back. Both of them went down hard in the street, the impact jolting every bone in Longarm's body. Momentum rolled him over a couple of times; then he came up on his hands and knees, fists clenched, ready to fight.

There was no one to trade punches with. Mercer lay flat on his back a couple of yards away, unmoving except for his mouth, which kept opening and closing although no sound came from his lips. His eyes were wide open.

Longarm got to his feet and went over to kneel at Mercer's side. Mercer's horrified gaze fastened on Longarm, and he said, "Can't . . . can't feel anything!"

Longarm saw then the odd angle at which Mercer's head was resting. The man's neck had broken when Longarm tackled him and both of them hit the ground so hard. That might have been his own neck, thought Longarm, had Mercer not hit the ground first and cushioned Longarm's landing.

"Your neck's broken, Leon," Longarm said. "No telling what else got busted up inside. You might as well tell me where those plates are. I'm going to find them anyway."

"In my . . . coat," sobbed Mercer.

Longarm reached inside the coat and found the plates in an inside pocket. He took them out and held them so that Mercer could see them. "Too many folks died because of these," he said, "including Janice Cassidy."

"I . . . I never meant for Janice to be hurt! We . . . we just wanted . . . to be rich!"

"Money ain't going to do you much good where you're going, Leon, not even real money. No telling how long you'll live, but I reckon you'll spend the rest of your days lying in a bed in a prison hospital, rotting away."

Even though Mercer couldn't move, his eyes seemed to reach up and clutch at Longarm. "Don't leave me like this, Long!" he pleaded. "Shoot me! Put a bullet through my brain!"

"Sorry, Leon," Longarm said as he stood up. "If you remember right, you took my guns. I couldn't shoot you now—even if I wanted to."

With that he turned and walked away, and behind him, Leon Mercer began to scream.

The sound went on for a long time.

Chapter 14

Longarm unwrapped the soft cloth from the bundle in his hands and laid the two rectangular pieces of metal on the desk in front of him. "There they are," he said. "That's what all the fuss was over."

Chief Marshal Billy Vail looked at the printing plates for a moment, then glanced up at Longarm. "Don't look like much to die for, do they?"

"Or to kill for," Longarm agreed as he sat down in the leather chair in front of Vail's desk. It was morning in Denver, the hands of the banjo clock on the wall resting at a little after ten o'clock. Longarm was damned tired, having been on the train all night. He felt grubby too, having come straight here to the Federal Building from the depot. He had wired most of the details of the case to Vail from Carson City, but he wanted to get those damned plates off his hands as soon as possible. As soon as he was finished here, he intended to head for his rented room on the other side of Cherry Creek and see if he could scare up a tub of hot water from his landlady. He wanted a nice long soak, eight or ten hours of sleep, and then maybe a bottle of Tom Moore. All those things might make him feel human again.

"I'll contact the families of the deputies who were killed in Albuquerque," said Vail as he put the printing plates into one of the drawers of his desk. "I want to let them know that the man responsible for their deaths is going to pay."

"Mercer'll be paying for a long time too," said Longarm. "The doc in Carson City said he ought to live, but he won't ever feel anything from the neck down again." A shudder ran through Longarm's rangy body. "There at the end he was begging me to shoot him, Billy. Maybe I should have."

"Hell, no," snapped Vail. "Leon Mercer used his position as Senator Padgett's assistant to set up a scheme that could have ruined the country's economy, not to mention being responsible for the deaths of several people. It would have been even worse if you and Miss Cassidy and that watchman hadn't made it out alive. Whatever happens to Mercer, he's got it coming."

Longarm chuckled. "I thought a lawman was supposed to be impartial, Billy."

"Impartial, hell," Vail said with a snort. He paused, then added, "By the way, Senator Padgett's still got a burr up his tail about the way you treated him. Good God, Custis, did you have to *slug* the man? He *is* a senator, you know."

Longarm took out a cheroot and rolled it between his fingers. "I explained all that to him back in Carson City. I was pretty sure he wasn't really mixed up in the counterfeiting, but I had to make it look good for Mercer. And if I'd been wrong about Padgett, well, then, he'd have been behind bars where he belonged. Don't see how anybody can be mad at me over that."

"Still, I think it would be a good idea if you made yourself scarce around Denver for a while."

Longarm sat up straight and said in an aggrieved tone, "Make myself scarce? Hell, Billy, I just got back!"

"I know that." Vail reached for one of the many documents scattered on his desk. "I've got an assignment here that's just right for you, though. There's a big ruckus over in Kansas, at a place called Hugoton."

Longarm held up his hands. "Just stop right there, Billy. You know I've never been one to shirk my responsibilities, but I've got something else I have to do first. I promised to escort a lady back to Missouri. Maybe I can stop by this place in Kansas on the way back and straighten 'em out."

"You're talking about Julie Cassidy?"

Longarm nodded solemnly. "After that stable collapsed, there was no way of telling if her sister died in the fire or from being trampled by that horse. All that really matters is that Janice betrayed Julie. That hurts mighty bad—but I reckon Julie still loved her anyway. It'll take some time for her to get over everything that happened."

"And you expect to help her get over it, I suppose."

"Don't you go leering about it, Billy Vail," Longarm warned sternly. "If you tell anybody I said it, I'll deny it, but I reckon I'd rather help Julie get back on to her feet—instead of off of 'em."

"Don't worry, Custis, your secret's safe with me." Vail shoved the documents aside. "All right, go to Missouri. I suppose you've earned it."

Longarm stood up. "Thanks, Billy."

He lit the cheroot as he left the Federal Building and turned toward Cherry Creek. It was true, he reflected—he was more interested in helping Julie get over her loss than he was in bedding her. "Maybe you're getting soft, old son," he muttered to himself.

And yet . . . sooner or later, Julie *would* be over Janice's death, and when that day came, she was liable to be mighty grateful to the fella who had helped her over the rough spots.

A grin began to spread over Longarm's face and his step grew a little jauntier as he walked toward home.

Watch for

LONGARM AND THE HOSTAGE WOMAN

215th novel in the bold LONGARM series
from Jove

Coming in November!

If you enjoyed this book, subscribe now and get...

TWO FREE

A $7.00 VALUE–

LONGARM

Explore the exciting Old West with
one of the men who made it wild!